DON'T

OBSESSIONS

A woman claiming to be Sam's wife threatens to turn Project Quantum Leap into a tabloid headline.

LOCH NESS LEAP

Sam makes a monster Leap into a physicist at Loch Ness—but the reason behind this mission is the real mystery . . .

HEAT WAVE

Sam must move fast to prove a man's innocence—while keeping peace in a town about to be torn apart by racial violence . . .

FOREKNOWLEDGE

Years ago, Sam Leaped into a criminal and sent her off to jail. Now she's free and wants revenge!

QUANTUM LEAP

OUT OF TIME. OUT OF BODY.
OUT OF CONTROL.

QUANTUM LEAP

SONG AND DANCE

A NOVEL BY

MINDY PETERMAN

BASED ON THE UNIVERSAL TELEVISION SERIES *QUANTUM LEAP* CREATED BY DONALD P. BELLISARIO

BERKLEY BOULEVARD BOOKS, NEW YORK

Quantum Leap: Song and Dance, a novel by Mindy Peterman, based on the Universal television series QUANTUM LEAP, created by Donald P. Bellisario.

QUANTUM LEAP: SONG AND DANCE

A Berkley Boulevard Book / published by arrangement with Universal Studios Publishing Rights, a Division of Universal Studios Licensing, Inc.

PRINTING HISTORY
Berkley Boulevard edition / October 1998

Cover illustration by Steve Gardner/Artworks.

The Penguin Putnam Inc. World Wide Web site address is
http://www.penguinputnam.com

Check out the Ace Science Fiction/Fantasy newsletter, and much more, at Club PPI!

ISBN: 0-425-16577-9

BERKLEY BOULEVARD
Berkley Boulevard Books are published by The Berkley Publishing Group, a member of Penguin Putnam Inc., 375 Hudson Street, New York, New York 10014.
BERKLEY BOULEVARD and its logo are trademarks belonging to Berkley Publishing Corporation.

PRINTED IN THE UNITED STATES OF AMERICA

10 9 8 7 6 5 4 3 2 1

This is for Courtney and Al, and Rudy the Dog

ACKNOWLEDGMENTS

Sincere thanks go to Ginjer Buchanan for encouraging me all these years, to Don Bellisario, Deborah Pratt, Scott Bakula, and Dean Stockwell for the inspiration; to Mary Tyler, Paul Cuticello, Phil Cutler, John Duenzel, Bob Briar, Lorraine Anderson, Jillian Webster, and Carol Davis for helping me keep the faith; and to Ellen Best and Joe Amarante for giving me a head start.

QUANTUM LEAP

SONG AND DANCE

CHAPTER ONE

"The artist is nothing without the gift, but the gift is nothing without work."

—Emile Zola

"Reality is merely an illusion, albeit a very persistent one."

—Albert Einstein

"You gonna eat it or paint a picture of it?"

The world-weary tone of the voice did nothing to make Sam want to rise out of the warmth of his cocoon and rejoin the land of the living. Moments ago, he'd been pure energy, drifting in a field of blue. Now that blue was betraying him, dissipating around his form quicker than he could say—

"Huh?"

"Stop giving me that dopey look. Are you gonna eat it or . . ."

By this time, Sam Beckett figured he should have had Leaping-in down to a science. Rule of thumb: if being spoken to at the time of arrival, give an immediate, coherent response. And if you don't succeed the first time, try, try again . . .

"Uh . . ." was the best he could do.

"You sound like a sick bear, Noah." The woman's brow furrowed, making her look a little like a confused chimp. "Are you gonna eat it?"

Sam blinked twice and chuckled, offering her his most charming grin. Still, she gave him no clue as to what "it" was. Might "it" be the brownish grapes or bruised apple in the cracked green bowl in the center of the table? Or could "it" be the half-eaten cracker she wielded in her hand? Or maybe, just maybe, "it" was the yellow monstrosity on the plate before him.

Ah, yes. Elementary, my dear Dr. Beckett . . .

"What is your problem? Look! Just look what's on your plate."

Sam lowered his gaze to again behold what had been placed before him.

"Mrs. Schmeltz gave me the recipe this afternoon and I promised her I'd surprise you by making it."

Sam tapped his fork against the food's brick-solid surface. "What is it?"

"What *is* it, you ask?" she ranted, throwing her hands up, appealing to the good Lord above. "It's noodle kugel, like you didn't know."

"Koo-gul?"

"Yes, yes." She shoved the remaining cracker in her

mouth, shaking her head as she chewed and swallowed. "What's the matter with you? You used to love kugel at the Wildwood Hotel. You couldn't get enough. Kugel, kugel, kugel. Breakfast, lunch and dinner. They had to bring it out for you special." She spread her arms out as if she were about to go into a dance. "Nothing was too good for Danny Ellman's son."

"I guess I don't remember," he muttered. "I was kind of young then."

"Not that young. If I recall correctly, your hormones had just about kicked in."

The familiar heat of embarrassment rose from his cheeks to his earlobes. If this was "his" mother, she was obviously not one to mince words about anything with her . . . son? He looked down, and was relieved to find himself clad in a man's sport shirt, work boots and dungarees. To make doubly sure he was of the male persuasion this time, he feigned an itch on his back, and was pleased to find no evidence of a bra strap. For this one sparkling moment, Sam was a very happy man.

When he was growing up on a farm in Indiana, sex had not been a subject broached on a daily basis. When Sam's father had finally gotten down to telling him the necessary facts of life (and only the necessary ones), Sam had already been primed on more than the basics from his older brother Tom. John Beckett's birds and the bees talk was at once painful and hilarious to recall. Even now, remembering all the fidgeting and blushing that went on while Dad gruffly stammered out the proper names of the male and female genitalia made him struggle to hold back a laugh. But he was glad for the recollection. It was always a welcome moment when the Swiss-cheese holes in his memory took a coffee break.

"That was the year I caught you taking that midnight

skinny-dip in the wading pool with Melissa Bauman.'' The woman chuckled, raking her fingers through her frizzy carrot-red hair. The shade was . . . amazing, one Lucy Ricardo would have cried for.

''Remember her, Noah?''

''Who . . . ?'' *Lucy?*

''Me-liss-a.''

He played along, grateful for this opportunity to let out his repressed laughter. ''How could I forget?'' Noah. She called him Noah. It was a good name, a survivor's name. Hell, he'd lived through worse drubbings than forty days and forty nights of rain.

''You should have married her. She came from money. Probably you'd've been better off.'' She grabbed a pack of Camels off the kitchen counter and pulled a cigarette out with her teeth. ''Try the kugel.''

Sam gave the yellow brick a disconsolate look. ''It's special. *You* should eat it.''

''I only had enough ingredients to make one piece.'' She jabbed the unlit cigarette at his plate. ''And I made it for you.''

She might be hurt if he refused. Pressing his thumb against the top of the kugel, Sam wondered if his teeth were up to the task at hand. After all, when was the last time he'd visited the dentist?

''Go on . . .''

Her look was too filled with anticipation for him to refuse. Scraping the tines of the fork across the top of the thick, wide, *hard* noodle, Sam held his breath, said a small silent prayer, then pressed down. *Cra-ack!* The kugel broke into a multitude of small jagged pieces. He winced at the mess, then looked slowly up at the woman. She stood frozen, demolished by disappointment, the Camel jittering between two upraised fingers. ''I made it just like she said.

It was easy.'' She frowned and hung her head. ''Too easy. I shoulda known when something's too easy, it's never any good.''

''It's . . . it's all right.'' He pushed back his chair and took two giant strides to the refrigerator. ''Look, I can make something for both of us.'' He pulled open the door. A chocolate bar, an open container of yogurt and more brown grapes stared back at him.

''You cook as well as me. Who're you kiddin'?'' She was rifling through her purse, tossing out balled-up tissues, creased photographs, two lipstick tubes and a broken pencil. ''Here.'' She shook out a badly wrinkled ten-dollar bill. ''It's all we have until my Social Security check comes tomorrow. If it's on time, that is. Damn mail.''

''No . . .''

''Whaddya mean no?''

''I can't take the last of your money.'' Sam's eyes traveled from the tired-looking bill to her careworn features. He hadn't noticed those wrinkles by the corners of her mouth before, or the creases on her neck and between her brow. She had seemed so young, so vibrant. Her violet skintight blouse and black stretch pants accentuated a youthful, well-cared-for body. But the passage of the years had taken its toll on her: too many defeats, too few triumphs. It was all there in her eyes.

She forced the money into his hand and closed his fingers around it. ''Go get Hop Joy's.''

''Hop Joy's?'' First kugel, now . . .

''Little Sir Echo, how do you do?'' she sang.

''Little Sir—''

''Chinese food, *bubelah*! Where is your mind today?''

''Ohhh. I don't . . . know. Well, at least let me pay.'' He threw the bill on the table then fished a beaten-looking wallet out of his pocket. ''It's the least I can—'' The wallet contained a yellowed receipt, two toothpicks in the dollar pocket and a driver's license.

"—do."

"You're busted, or did you forget?"

"No . . . I didn't . . ."

"I thought for a minute you'd been holding out on me. You got some bills stashed somewhere?"

Sam looked at her hard. "Not that I know of."

"Your unemployment check arrives on Tuesday." She hitched a thumb at herself proudly. "I keep track of these things."

Not wanting to stick around long enough to shove his foot in his mouth again, Sam pocketed the money and found what he thought to be the apartment door. It was, in fact, the pantry. Two cans of sardines greeted him from the second shelf.

"No-ah!"

Gathering his determination and gritting his teeth, he swerved around and headed for the small, sparsely furnished living room. Almost immediately, he stumbled into the apartment door. Congratulating himself, he twisted the knob, but it refused to budge. With a grunt, he tried again. No luck. The woman moved to his side, watching his efforts with barely restrained amusement. "Noah, honey." She grinned, patted his hand, then brought it down to his side. "It only opens if you unlock it."

"Right . . . Mom."

She twisted the lock to a horizontal position, turned the knob and pushed open the door. "Voilà!" Smiling, Sam gave her a jaunty salute and headed out. He was then introduced to another piece of Noah's world: the dank hallway, its green paint flaking and peeling, the heavy stench of broiled fish and cigarettes making the air almost unbreathable. He held his breath and raced down the two flights of stairs, praying very hard for the Chinese restaurant to find him.

CHAPTER TWO

The girl stared at Rebecca, waiting.

"Deep breath," Rebecca said, her lips set apart in an anticipatory grin. "Feel it right in here." She touched one finger to the spot between the girl's tummy and torso. "Always keep in mind, this is where you sing from. Not here." She brought the finger up to tap the girl's throat. "Now . . . do the scale again for me, okay?"

The girl nodded and stood even straighter, fingering her multicolored beads as if they were the magical components of a good luck talisman. "Do, re, mi, fa, so, la, ti, do," she sang in a crisp bell-like voice as Rebecca played a middle C scale on the upright piano.

"Terrific, Betsy. Did you feel the difference?"

Betsy's eyes lit up. "Yup."

"Did you hear the difference?"

"In-doobitably!"

Rebecca playfully chucked Betsy under her small round chin. "You've got that callback coming in a couple of days. I think you're ready. How do you feel about it?"

"Pretty confident." Betsy bounced slightly on her toes, her eyes as bright as Rebecca knew her future would be.

"Soon you'll be wowin' them on Broadway, even if it's not this time. Then you won't even remember me." She pouted and rubbed one eye, feigning tears.

"I'll thank you in the *Playbill*, Rebecca. Just wait and see. And if they let me, I'll introduce you from the audience."

She smoothed the girl's hair, then moved to the piano and closed the lid. Her temples throbbed; her heart was a ten-ton stone inside her chest, its relentless pounding reminding her of who she was and what her life was really about. Being with Betsy and the others always made her forget. They looked up to her. To them she was special. But they were only children. They'd grow older, see the real person behind the attractive woman with the pale pretty face and even prettier voice. Then they'd know . . .

"What's wrong, Rebecca?" The child had donned her Elton John sweatshirt. She clasped her music to her chest, tilting her head in concern.

A smile crept across Rebecca's face. "I was thinking very hard about all the lovely music you're going to make. And when I think hard like that . . . I guess I look kind of serious."

"My mom says it's not good to frown. Gives you wrinkles round your mouth." Betsy twirled around and pulled open the front door. "See you next week."

Leaning against the piano, Rebecca gave a small wave

and watched the door hiss shut. Last year she had installed an automatic door closer, since kids being kids loved to race out after lessons, unmindful of how hard the door slammed after them. This way, she didn't have to cluck at them about it like an old mother hen. She used to hate it when her mother badgered her about inconsequential things like door slamming and not wiping your feet, making them seem like the most heinous crimes imaginable. Life was too short . . .

Betsy's heels made tiny scritching noises against the pavement as she skipped down the block. Pulling the heavy taupe drapes open an inch, Rebecca was just in time to see her turn the corner and disappear from view. She would have loved to turn the corner with her, and bask in the lovely September twilight. But just the thought of it turned her palms to ice and made her heart race triple time.

To calm herself, she took three deep breaths and sat at the edge of her thickly cushioned sofa, surveying what had been her world for the past two years. It was a warm, comfortable domain—she'd made sure of it. To the right of the piano, hardcover books and photographs of some past and present students lined the wood-paneled wall. A ficus tree sat in the corner by the window. Some days she dared to draw back a corner of the curtain and allow the tree to bathe in the sunlight's warmth. She wished she could enjoy the light too, but she couldn't. She couldn't. When she was younger, she loved the sun, the open sky. Now she retreated from them, hiding in her bedroom with her records and her novels, until hunger or another appointment forced her out again.

Grocery stores delivered for a modest service charge; mail-order catalogues offered anything, everything. She had survived quite well, very well. People would be surprised. If they knew.

Through the corner of her eye she spied the riot of paperwork on her desk. She had never managed to become the organized person her mother spent years training her to be. But she was a success, regardless, wasn't she? Take that, Mom! Huffing out a laugh, she marveled at her professional good fortune, then abruptly wondered why the rest of her life was not equally charmed.

The phone peeked out from beneath the two pages of her student roster. A pink Post-it note with Noah Ellman's phone number scrawled on it was taped to the dial. He hadn't returned her call yet. In a way she was relieved. If she hired him, he'd have to work here every day. They'd be in each other's company for hours at a time. Quite possibly, he'd see more of her than his own family. After a while she might slip up, get too comfortable with him. In time, he might suspect her secret. After a long while, he would know.

Was it really necessary to hire someone? Sighing, she stole another look at the mess. If it hadn't been for *New York* magazine doing that feature story on her, making the whole town aware of how she'd given voice training to some of the most successful young performers around, she wouldn't be in this dilemma.

It had been easy to dismiss the majority of applicants who had responded to her *New York Times* classified ad. She could convince herself of anything, given the chance. This one was too chatty, this one too serious, might put off the kids, this one just didn't . . . look right. But Noah Ellman—he was sweet, qualified, musical, and a bit on the shy side. After scrutinizing his application, calling his references, waiting for the negative words that never came, she stopped trying to find something wrong. He was the one.

Now if he would just take her calls, they'd be in business.

Noah's mother, Gerda, had been fielding Rebecca's calls, and since their first hello, they'd become telephone compadres. Gerda Ellman had that tough New York grit about her; her attitude was one Rebecca strived for but could never affect. She wished she could be strong like Gerda and let life roll off her shoulders. The three times they'd spoken, Noah was not home, but Gerda promised to ''wring his neck'' if he didn't call her back as soon as he got in. This had been going on for two days. Noah's neck must be twisted like a pretzel by now. She supposed she should try again, if for no other reason than to have a few laughs with Gerda, then play the waiting game one more time. And what if Noah didn't respond this time? *What'll you do then, hotshot?*

Had she scared him off by playing Boss Lady? she wondered, walking to the desk. Had she come on too strong, bombarding him with questions? He hadn't *seemed* flustered by her manner, sitting relaxed on the sofa, replying to her edgy queries in a soft, calm tone.

With one swipe of her hand, she cleared the mess and pulled the note off the telephone. She stared at the number for a few moments, tracing each digit with her forefinger, then grabbed the phone, settled onto the sofa again. And dialed.

CHAPTER THREE

The Chinese restaurant did find Sam. It waved to him from the end of the block, its sign blinking red and yellow, jutting out from the storefront like a flag. "Hop Joy's Chinese Food, Hop Joy's . . ."

He strode toward it, relief washing over him with every step. At least now the woman would be assured a decent dinner. An image of the watery yogurt languishing in the nearly empty refrigerator popped into his head, but he quickly pushed the thought away. Tonight he would buy her something really special with the ten dollars, even if it meant going without supper himself. The woman didn't deserve to be disappointed twice in one evening. Why couldn't Mrs. Schmeltz have given her the recipe yesterday? The real Noah might have handled the fiasco with a lot more finesse. And she deserved much better than a shabby walk-up in a seedy part of whatever this town was. Sam had an inkling she was pretty tough emotionally, relying on her sense of humor to smooth over the rough spots in her life. What had brought her here? he wondered. It couldn't have always been this way . . .

''Pretty sky.''

Sam's heart lurched, the gravelly voice jolting him from his reverie. He whipped around, stumbling over his own feet and grasping the lip of a garbage can to break his fall.

''*Al!*''

''You know, twilight was always my favorite time of the day.'' The hologram puffed his cigar and cocked his head, contemplating the sky. ''You can make so many interesting suggestions to a woman at twilight and she'll agree to them every time. I think it's all those bee-yoo-tiful colors: purples and golds and fiery oranges. A soothing voice and a romantic backdrop can hypnotize a woman into doing . . . some lovely things. But don't try making those suggestions in the middle of the afternoon. All you get is a good crack across the face.'' His mouth twitched. ''I know.''

''Al-l.'' Sam was still clinging to the can.

The hologram bounced on the balls of his feet, his purple jacket with the gray trim complementing the colors of twilight. He tapped his smoldering cigar twice and surveyed the silent streets. ''Dinnertime in Brooklyn, New York. Everyone's home chowing down on homemade pasta, or kugel, or gefilte fish—''

''Did you say kugel?'' Sam asked, continuing his walk.

''Sure.'' Al drifted to his side. ''Noodle kugel. My second . . . no, my third wife, Ruthie, used to make it for me all the time. It was good stuff, but the pasta had to be soft or else—''

"The kugel gets hard as a brick." Sam stopped in his tracks and shook an accusatory finger at Al. "You've been spying on me. The woman in that apartment back there tried to feed me kugel. It was hard as a rock."

"Then it was baked too long." Al feigned a hurt look. "And I wasn't spying on you. I just know what life is like in Brooklyn. Ruthie's parents lived here. Between her mother's cooking and hers, I've downed enough kugel to last me a lifetime."

They reached the entrance to Hop Joy's. Business was not booming. Through the plate glass window, Sam could see two elderly Asian men playing cards at a wooden table by the door. The lone customer, a middle-aged woman with strawberry blond hair, sat at a table near the counter. Immersed in her paperback, she was doing a passable job of using chopsticks to eat her fried rice. Behind the counter, an apple-cheeked woman, her hair jet black, her skin the color of milky tea, stirred a steaming pot of food at the stove. Sam entered, Al melting through the glass behind him. "Spanish Eyes" bleated from a transistor radio on a shelf behind the cash register. One of the card players hummed along.

"Something smells great." Sam scanned the menu printed on the wall above the counter. Through the corner of his eye he noticed the woman at the table looking at him over the top of her glasses. When he turned to meet her gaze, she delved back into her book. Again, he scanned the menu, and again, he caught her surreptitious stare.

"Hello," he said, while turning toward her, so she had no chance of escaping back into the words.

Flustered, she dropped her chopsticks into her rice.

"Uh . . . is that good?" he asked.

She stopped chewing, her gaze flitting from her book to her food.

"I'm sorry. I meant what you're eating. Is it good?"

The woman swallowed, then frowned, gravely studying the contents of her plate.

"It's just that I've never been here before and I was wondering what to get . . ."

Slowly she allowed herself to meet his eyes and gave him a hesitant grin. "I thought I recognized you. You're Noah, Gerda's son."

Al checked the handlink. "Bin-go, Sam. She's right."

"You were here with your mom just last week." The woman removed the chopsticks from the rice and wiped them clean with a napkin.

"I was . . ."

"Maybe you forgot." She shrugged and dug into her rice again.

"No . . . no. What I meant to say is that . . . Mom usually comes here on her own to get food for herself, since . . . I'm not home much. The day I was with her she was just getting some rice . . . for herself. So, you see, I've never been here to order a meal before . . . by myself." He forced a chuckle, giving Al a wild-eyed *help me out here* look.

"Pretty fair catch, Sam." Al said. "But you've done better."

"All the food here is good," she said, wiping her chin with her napkin. "Stick to the combination plates, though. You get the best value with the combination plates." She gave him a serious look, then went back to her reading.

"Thanks." He gazed up at the menu with renewed confidence. The prices were very reasonable but the combination plates did seem to give the most for the money. He could buy two dinners and still manage to bring home some change. Only problem was, he had no idea what "Mom" liked to eat.

"Chow mein, Sam. Look at that. You get pork fried rice,

spare ribs, soup and chicken chow mein for two bucks. You can't beat it.''

''I'll have that,'' Sam said to the woman still stirring the contents of the pot.

''What you have, mister?'' She tapped the metal spoon against the pot. ''This wonton soup. Fresh made.''

''Good. I'll have two number ones with . . . uh the wonton soup.''

''Fifteen minutes.''

''Good choice, Sam,'' Al said, leading the way out the door.

Sam moved to follow, but paused in mid-step, then doubled back to the woman's table. ''Enjoy the rest of your dinner.''

''Oh.'' She closed her book, a well-worn copy of *Gone With the Wind*, holding her place with her thumb. ''Please tell your mom that Mary Jane Wax says hello.''

''Sure.'' He smiled. ''No problem.'' If the situation were different, if he didn't have to find out all the particulars as to why he was here, he would have invited Mary Jane Wax to spend some time with ''Mom'' and himself.

''Come on, Sam.'' Al called from outside, one forefinger beckoning through the glass.

The good smells stayed with Sam as he followed his Observer outside. To the left, a weatherbeaten green bench called to him. He sat, strctching his legs, as Al tapped the handlink. The link's keys squawked, its colors blinking like casino lights.

''Le-et's see. It's Monday, September twenty-fifth, nineteen seventy eight. You are Noah Ellman, twenty-eight years old, divorced five years, unemployed three months.''

Sam hitched his elbows over the back of the bench and exhaled softly. ''Great.''

''Well, it's not your fault you're divorced. Not really,

anyway. Your wife got disco fever and ran off with a roadie for K.C. and the Sunshine Band."

"Kay Cee?"

"Yeah, you remember. Disco." Al pumped his hips, holding the link to his lips like a microphone. "There was nothing better than bumping and grinding to K.C.'s hits. 'That's the Way I Like It.' 'Shake, Shake, Shake Your Booty.' Oooh, yeah!"

Smirking, Sam shook his head. "Sorry, I don't remember."

"It figures you'd forget the quality stuff." Al sighed and poked at the handlink. "And it's not your fault you're unemployed. Noah was the manager of Berlloff's Music Store on Kings Highway up until three months ago when the place lost its lease." The link squealed, spewing the data. "Unfortunately, his apartment was in the same building as the store, and when the rent was raised, he was forced to move in with his mother, Gerda."

"That's who I just ordered the chow mein for?"

"Right." Al nodded. "Now, even though Noah's situation is no great shakes, Ziggy doesn't think you're here for him."

"I'm here for Gerda."

"Yeah."

Sam slipped a look through the window to see if any of the card players, the cook or Mary Jane was aware of his seemingly one-sided conversation. It was too easy to get immersed in what Al was saying and end up looking like a total fool (or worse). This time, it seemed, he was safe. The men were engrossed in their game, the woman cradled a phone receiver to her ear while ladling soup into a Styrofoam bowl, and Mary Jane was deeply involved with Scarlet and Rhett.

"So what's Gerda's story, Al? She doesn't get killed or anything . . ."

"Killed?" Al knitted his brow and regarded the link. "No. Death by disappointment, maybe."

Thinking of Gerda in her sad little apartment with the bruised fruit caused Sam to wince as if he'd been struck.

"You like her, huh?" Al regarded Sam with a half smile.

"She's . . . interesting, sad. I think she deserves a lot better than what she's got."

Al shrugged. "Most people on this earth deserve better. But Gerda's case might not be so tough to remedy."

"What do I have to do?"

"You've gotta help make her a star."

Sam dropped his arms to his sides and gave Al a look of weary tolerance. "That's going to save her life?"

"Well . . . it could."

"Now I'm a casting agent."

Al took a long drag on his Havana. "Uh-uh, Sam. Just listen."

"I'm all ears."

"Gerda Ellman was married to Danny Ellman, a philandering trumpet player who worked the Catskill Mountain resort circuit in upstate New York. It was no secret he was bed hopping, but Gerda stayed with him and got pregnant with you . . . Noah. After Noah was born, Gerda performed in some of the revues in the resort hotels, to augment the pittance Danny threw her way when he felt like it. She really enjoyed the business, but taking care of Noah was her main priority. Unfortunately, Danny's boozing and carousing were his priorities, and they finally did him in. He was only forty-two when he was found dead of a heart attack in a showgirl's bed."

"Not a very proud legacy."

"Danny Ellman was a swine." Al's lip curled in disgust.

"He borrowed against his insurance policy, and gambled the money away. And Gerda and Noah were left with zippo when he kicked." The constant flicker of the link could not hide the anger in Al's dark eyes. "Gerda had to waitress to make ends meet and never got to work onstage again. And it's a shame because according to the write-ups in the *Monticello Gazette*, she was pretty damn good. Here's one from August tenth, nineteen fifty-three. 'Gerda Ellman has a voice as strong as Merman's. Her "Lullaby of Broadway" number brought down the house.' "

"It's too bad, Al." Sam spread his hands and hitched his shoulders. "But what am I supposed to—"

"Two months ago, Gerda signed up to audition for a nationally televised talent show called 'You Can Be a Star.' The audition's four nights from now, but her dancing partner's not gonna show, which is going to disqualify her. She's so brokenhearted that she dies of heart failure watching the TV show she probably would have performed on."

"She might not have made the cut, Al." Sam watched the hologram pace.

"She never even had the chance to try." He wagged a finger in Sam's face. "You've gotta make sure she does."

"Who's her partner?"

Al's fingers flew over the keypad. He glared at it a moment, then whacked it on its side, which caused it to squeal like a trapped rat. "No data, Sam. Those records were tossed a long time ago. All we have is a winner's list."

"I'll have to find out who he is from Gerda, then talk to the guy, make sure he shows." Sam tapped his chin, and raised his eyes past the rooftops toward the first glimmer of starlight. "Or . . ." He hitched a brow. "I could take his place."

"Sam, I don't think—"

"I could, you know." Sam rubbed his palms together, then shook a finger at his friend. "It wouldn't take me that long to learn the steps."

"Sam." Al bounced on his toes and raised his eyebrows at the restaurant window.

"It wouldn't be a problem. All I'd have to do would be to get her to let me help her practice. Then—"

"*Sam!*"

Sam's mouth was still open, tongue poised to shape his next word as he followed Al's gaze toward the window. Quite a crowd had gathered. The cardplayers had laid down their hands, and now offered him toothsome, nervous grins. Mary Jane stood beside them, *Gone With the Wind* under her right arm, pocketbook slung over her left shoulder. She blinked at him somberly from behind her lenses. The young woman behind the counter dangled a brown paper bag in one hand. Her smile was halfhearted, weary, as if she'd seen it all, and a looney guy jabbering to himself outside her restaurant wasn't going to put a dent in her evening.

"I know you're a good dancer, Sam, but Ziggy says your priority is to make sure Gerda's partner shows. And I think she might be right."

Sam pushed off the bench and swerved past the hologram toward the door and the gaggle of curious onlookers. He sighed, thinking Al and Ziggy were probably on the mark. What if he sweated to learn the routine and his efforts brought the same results? What good would he have done Gerda then? Thoughts racing, he tightened his lips and grasped the door handle. "I'll make sure the guy shows," Sam said softly. "Even if I have to drag him to the audition myself."

He stepped into the restaurant, doing his best to ignore the stares. But he couldn't ignore Mary Jane Wax, who walked beside him to the counter. "Don't feel bad. There's nothing wrong with talking to yourself, Noah." She blushed. "I do it all the time."

"You do?"

"Four sixty-three." The cook held her hand out for the money, and Sam placed the rumpled ten inside it. The register rang as she opened the cash drawer, then she handed Sam his change.

"I've been told it's a sign of intelligence."

Sam gave her a tired grin as he grasped the bag of food and pocketed the bills. "Thanks, Mary Jane. I was afraid you thought I was some kind of nut."

For the first time, she really looked at him. "I think . . . sometimes you have to give in to a little craziness to preserve your sanity."

He nodded, smile broadening, thinking, *Yeah, if she only knew . . .*

CHAPTER FOUR

Sam bounded up the stairs to the Ellmans' apartment, thankful that the wonderful scents of garlic and spices coming from the Hop Joy's bag sufficiently masked the sad, stale smells in the hallway. It felt good bringing home the food. It made him feel as though he'd . . . accomplished something. Never mind the fact it was Gerda's money he had used, or that she could have just as easily gone to Hop Joy's herself. In the space of a half hour, he had made life a little easier for her. *At least*, he thought, *I'm heading in the right direction.*

He slowed his steps, pausing at the second-floor landing. A woman was singing, her strong alto drifting down from the floor above. The voice was the same one he'd heard while walking home. Then he'd thought it was coming from someone's radio, blaring out an open window. But no. It's Gerda, Sam thought. It's Gerda belting some tune about moonin' and spoonin'. Sam leaned against the railing, head cocked, not wanting to go upstairs just yet and spoil the moment. Her voice reminded Sam of one of those Broadway divas Ed Sullivan used to feature on his shows. If things had gone differently, if Danny Ellman hadn't been such a . . . louse, Gerda Ellman might have ended up as one of those "queens of the stage," as Ed liked to call them.

He should go. The food was getting cold. She would ask him why he took so long, then he'd have to go through the trouble of making up an excuse. Fascinated, he continued to listen. "In a minute," he whispered. "Just till the song ends." Her singing exemplified her strength, her will to endure. He couldn't allow one disappointment to rob her of that. After all she had been through, raising Noah alone, living on tips and scraps, she was still able to belt out a tune and pretend the years hadn't passed her by. In her dreams she was still knockin' 'em dead in the Catskills, giving Merman some hefty competition.

She was really letting loose now, her song causing the wooden bannister to tremble against Sam's hip. Shifting the bag to his other hand, he wondered if the neighbors ever complained. She'd probably tell them to "shove it sideways . . . with a hot poker," if they ever dared. Noting how no one was opening a door to complain, he figured that at some point she already had told them that.

The song was coming to its bombastic finish as Sam reached the third floor. Easing open the apartment door, he stepped inside to see Gerda with her back to him, emoting before the full-length mirror on the wall by the kitchen. Throwing her arms in the air, she performed a one-two hip shot and gave the last line everything she had: "... by the silvery moo-OO-oon!"

He set the bag on a rickety end table, then gave her a round of enthusiastic applause, garnished with whistles and hoots.

Turning, she set her hands on her hips. The scoop-neck collar of her shirt was soaked with sweat. "Well?"

Sam continued to applaud. "That was great."

"No-ah!"

His hands fell to his sides, the displeasure in her eyes stopping him cold.

"Could you hear me?" she asked.

"Sure, I could hear you. The whole building could hear you."

She scrubbed two hands through her hair and grumbled, "Talking to you is like pulling teeth."

What now? What the hell did I do n—

"Noah. Baby. Lightness and sweetness of my life. What is the question I always ask you when you come back from Hop Joy's?"

Sam rubbed his palms together, willing himself not to give in to temptation and walk out the door. "You . . . ask me if I heard you."

"Very good. I ask you if you heard me . . . where?" She thrust her chin at him and raised her brows.

Suddenly the light went on. "Outside?"

"Goo-ood."

"Yes, I did. Actually, I thought it was someone's radio."

"Then I'll have to practice harder, Noah." She tapped her chin as she stared his way, but Sam didn't think she was looking at him at all. Her mind was somewhere else. Maybe she was back on stage at the Wildwood Hotel, or maybe she had flashed forward to the brighter lights of TV stardom.

''But you sounded great,'' he told her again.

She took one step toward him, her brown eyes wide, her fingers splayed against her chest. ''Honey, when your mom sings, everybody has to know it's me, flesh and blood, not some radio broadcast. This is Gerda's law. If I ever hope to raise the roof off the Starlight Ballroom, I have to start with making the foundation rattle here.''

Sam touched his hip, recalling the buzz of the wooden bannister against it. ''I think you did that.''

''I have to be ready.'' She suddenly became very interested in her ring, twisting the small purple stone on her right middle finger around and around. ''I can't show up unprepared.''

''You're hardly slacking off, Mom.'' Sam raised a forefinger. Here was an opening. He would ask her about the audition, get the ball rolling. Easy . . .

''What's to eat?'' Gerda grabbed the paper bag off the table and swept past him into the kitchen.

In the few moments it took Sam to follow, she had most of the white cardboard cartons lined up on the table, the brown paper bag crumpled beneath her slippered toe. The table had been set economically but with care: pink floral paper napkins, matching paper plates and cups, plastic forks, knives and spoons. It reminded Sam of a kid's birthday party. All that was missing was the cake, the hats . . .

''*Noah!*''

But not the noisemakers.

''Yes, Mom.''

She foraged through a carton with a plastic knife. ''What the hell is *this*?'' Her mouth puckered as if she'd just sucked a lemon.

Eyebrows raised, he leaned over the container and stared at the flaccid chicken strips and vegetables mixed with the thick opaque sauce. "Chow mein," he replied. "Chicken . . . chow mein."

"Feh!" She pushed it toward him and began spooning rice from another carton into her plate. "What did you think, I suddenly changed my eating habits?"

"Well . . . I didn't. What I mean is I . . ." He paused, took a deep breath, then blurted out, "Mary Jane Wax said everything at Hop Joy's was good."

Gerda's hand holding the spoon froze between the carton and her plate. "Where did you see her?"

"At Hop Joy's."

"Was she alone?"

Sam nodded.

"Figures. No matter what I tell her," Gerda muttered, "she never listens."

"She seemed pretty content reading *Gone With the Wind* and eating her dinner." Sam shrugged. "A little lonely, maybe."

"Pah! A person's only lonely by choice. Her husband died over a year ago. A year! She has no excuse for spending so much time on her own. There are plenty of fish in the sea." Gerda set down the spoon and dumped the remaining rice onto her plate.

"Really . . . ?"

She wrinkled her nose at the steam rising from the chow mein container. "Sometimes I think your mind's in outer space somewhere. Chicken chow mein. I hate that stuff."

"I'm sorry." He looked down at the cracked linoleum and ran a finger across the back of the wooden chair.

"Next time, fried rice. Think. Use the brains God gave you." *Use the brains God gave you.* The expression was one Thelma Beckett used now and then. Sam recalled it drifting from his mother's lips as a loving admonishment, like a lesson from Aesop's Fables. So far, other than the fact they were of the same gender, it was about the only thing Gerda and his mother had in common.

"Okay, honey?" she asked.

He quirked a smile. "Okay."

She picked up two spareribs and set them straight and neat by her rice, like soldiers at attention. "Eat, Noah. Your chow mein's getting cold."

He *was* hungry. Stomach groaning, he sat across from her and spooned a small mound of rice onto his plate. After burying it under two large dollops of chow mein, he stirred the mixture well, then raised a forkful to his lips.

"She called again," Gerda said through a mouthful of food.

"Who?" The forkful of chow mein was just a tease, an enticing, dangling prize he was obviously not meant to enjoy. He lowered it slowly, heaving a silent sigh, belly grumbling in protest.

"Who? How many 'shes' call you, Noah? Do you have a harem I don't know about?"

"No . . . I don't think so . . ."

"Rebecca Wexler!" she exclaimed, as if the name were the correct response to the twenty-five-thousand-dollar question. She shook a sparerib at him, then began to nibble on it.

"Oh."

She swallowed, and her lips twisted in annoyance. "Oh-hh! Is that all you can say?"

Sam drummed his fingers against the table, watching his food cool and congeal, steeling himself for another sardonic salvo.

"Rebecca Wexler has only been calling you every day since the interview."

Interview? As in job interview? His head jerked up. "I guess . . . it must have slipped my mind."

"Oooh, how convenient." Shaking her head, she dabbed soy sauce from a little plastic packet onto her rice. "When it suits you to remember, you do. If one of your fair-weather friends called about going to the movies or the disco or bowling, you'd remember, wouldn't you?"

"Disco . . ." Sam cringed.

She shoved a forkful of rice in her mouth, chewing and swallowing, not missing a beat. "Where are those 'friends' since you got laid off, huh? Not one of them even offered to put you up when you had no place to go."

"I guess they knew I had you, Mom." Sam smiled sweetly. She was lambasting Noah, of course, not him. And from what he could gather, maybe the guy deserved it.

"How very, very convenient." She sipped her water, then scrubbed the grease off her lips with her napkin. "You are so full of shit, Noah. Rebecca Wexler calls every day, offering you a job, and you won't even give her the courtesy of a reply."

He sighed. *Help me out here. Someone* . . . Folding his arms on the table, he set his lips in a tight line and met her glare.

"I know what your problem is," she said, setting her fork on her plate.

"You do."

"I do."

"And that is . . ."

"Noah, my darling . . . ," Gerda said, mimicking Sam's saccharine smile from moments before. "You are scared out of your skivvies."

CHAPTER FIVE

"Ziggy?"

"Yes, Gooshie."

"Would you . . . run down everything for me . . . one more time?"

The hybrid computer's elongated silence was the closest she would ever come to heaving an exasperated sigh. Dr. Beckett had not programmed her for such blatant humanisms. But her tolerant, albeit condescending, comprehension of human emotions would be part of her until she was "stripped down for junk metal," as the admiral might say. The unfortunate fact was that she *did* feel; at times she became depressed, snide, boastful, irritatingly prideful. But she never failed to maintain an appreciable intellectual distance between herself and her human cohabitants. She would never allow her feelings to equate her with . . . them, and treated those Beckett-given emotions as necessary, but unwanted, appendages. Gooshie couldn't help thinking that if Ziggy could have devised a way of divorcing herself from them, she most certainly would have by now.

"Would you like a printout, or would you just like me to relay the facts to you?"

Dr. Irving Gushman, or Gooshie, as Al had dubbed him the first day at the project, leaned forward behind his console, setting his chin in his hands. "Just . . . tell me, Ziggy." He closed his eyes. Ursula and Fred, the two techs who usually worked by his side, had gone to lunch. Actually, Gooshie asked them to go, even though it was only eleven-thirty. Since the first few tidbits of data had scrolled across the console's monitors hours before, Gooshie had wanted to be alone. At some point, he'd dismissed his assistants, despite their protestations at leaving him by himself. The standard routine was for them to take shifts or call in a tech from a different department if an all-nighter was imminent. Gooshie thanked them for their concern, and walked them to the door, not seating himself again until he was sure they had gone. He didn't want anyone to see him this way. During the early morning hours, he managed to lay his head on the cool fiberglass console and take a catnap, order three salami, onion and Swiss cheese hoagies from the commissary and prod Ziggy countless times to see if her data had changed. It hadn't.

Ziggy wasn't lying. She didn't know how. It was another humanism Dr. Beckett had not blessed her with. At this moment, Gooshie almost wished he had. At least then there would be another explanation . . .

Ziggy.

She was more a part of him than anyone could know. In

some ways she was as much his baby as Dr. Beckett's. He rocked back in his chair and closed his eyes. If the doctor was Ziggy's father, Gooshie mused, and Al her uncle, perhaps he was Cousin Gooshie—the intellectual, slightly off-kilter relative who was secretly her favorite.

"Are you awake, Gooshie? I'm sure you are aware that I cannot read your brainwaves."

Lifting his head, he blinked at the multicolored strobe on the wall that housed the essence of what made Ziggy . . . what she was: a sampling of Dr. Beckett's brain tissue, and a bit of the admiral's thrown in for good measure.

But it was Gooshie's hands on the keys. "Yes, Ziggy, please begin."

"Dr. Beckett has Leaped into Noah Ellman, son of Gerda Ellman and the late Daniel Ellman. Gerda and Noah reside at 1403 Flatbush Avenue, Brooklyn, New York. The date is September twenty-fifth, nineteen seventy-eight . . ."

She continued, her voice rolling off the walls and ceilings in its calm, mellifluous fashion. The data was the same. Nothing had changed. Nothing at all. He had heard right the first, second and third times. The whole unfortunate scenario was right on the mark. And everything about it was very, very wrong.

He swallowed hard. "This is not happening, Ziggy."

"On the contrary, Gooshie, since Dr. Beckett has Leaped into Noah Ellman in nineteen seventy-eight, it *is* happening . . . to him. Which means whatever he eventually alters will affect us and a faction of the world's populace to some degree. If you like, I can discuss some examples of the 'domino' effects of Dr. Beckett's travels—"

"No, thank you, Ziggy," he said and took a breath, pressing his fists against his eyelids. Explosions of red, green and purple appeared like fireworks on black velvet.

''Can you theorize how events might change within the next forty-eight hours?''

''No. Dr. Beckett has only altered minute factions of the original history, so far. It is too soon to tell.''

Gooshie's eyes ached. He set his fists on the console, and the pain eased. ''Thank you, Ziggy,'' he rasped.

''You're welcome, Gooshie.''

Ziggy's voice was gentle, tinged with concern, which was unlike her. Perhaps the computer was empathizing with his melancholia. No. Gooshie knew he was reading more into her tone than what was really there. Strip away that dose of human spirit entwined with the circuits and floppies and all you had was a few hundred buckets of steel, plastic and wire. Yet the symbiosis Gooshie had developed with Ziggy was something he coveted, enjoyed. He looked forward to bantering with her, discussing the complexities of scenarios, witnessing through her words the altering of events from (most of the time) wrong to right, tragedy to triumph. For Gooshie, watching the Leaps unfold via Ziggy's expositions was the ultimate in vicarious living.

And Gooshie was an old pro at living life through something or someone else, be it a slightly racy movie, books, the Project techs' ramblings (which usually had something to do with girlfriends, boyfriends or vacation hot spots). There was much he had missed out on, he supposed, but he was long past caring. He was one of those rare people satisfied with his existence. Except for Dr. Beckett's dilemmas and the admiral's occasional tirade, his life was practically stress free. For this reason, Gooshie welcomed the occasional ''fly in the ointment.'' It was the ''spice on the pudding'' that made living a touch more interesting, as his mother used to say. But now Time, Fate, or Whoever had decided to get into the act and smother the pudding with a ladleful of tabasco.

"Why?" he moaned, eyes rolling toward the shadows playing across the acoustical tiles on the ceiling.

Suddenly, it was as if the room were closing in on him. He could imagine the ceiling lowering itself inches at a time, until it was close enough to touch him, close enough to crush him. Breathing hard, he felt his heart knock against his ribs. Nine stories above was the New Mexico dust bowl, littered with scrub brush and little else. Sometimes he fantasized that the entire planet was a desert, its sole inhabitants Project personnel. Their job was to look out for Sam, who was off in that other world—the one with all the people.

A noise that straddled the line between a snuffle and a laugh escaped him. *You pathetic man. You pathetic little man.* He wrapped his fingers around his padded armrest to still their trembling. He wasn't going to make it through this Leap. If he had to sit here listening to Ziggy spout Dr. Beckett's progress, hour after hour, day after day, until the Leap's inevitable conclusion, Beeks would have to cart him off to the infirmary—wrapped up tight in one of those industrial-strength straitjackets.

She would throw all kinds of questions at him about his very un-Gooshie-like behavior. But he wouldn't tell her anything, which would make the situation worse. His fingers fumbled at his mustache, the scene playing out in vivid Technicolor in his head. Verbeena would not relent, her liquid brown eyes seeing through the facade of the pathetic little man to the very core of his soul. Gooshie had observed her work with the visitors in the Waiting Room, and knew he was no match for her. She would dig and dig and dig until she found the mother lode, the secret. He would crumble. But worse than that, she would know why.

His only option was to leave the project for a while. Two weeks should suffice. He pushed out of his chair and stood behind it, swiveling it back and forth with his hand. Staying away until this Leap was over would afford him time to regain his inner calm, keeping everyone's favorite nebbishy cousin on an even keel.

Two weeks.

His head jerked up. A sprightly waterfall of laughter interrupted his thoughts. Ursula and Fred entered the room like they were just strolling in from a date. Taking a deep breath, he cast them his very best Gooshie grin. "Did you . . . have an enjoyable lunch?"

Ursula stopped in mid-ramble. They stared at Gooshie, as if his presence were an unexpected intrusion. "It was okay." She shrugged. "A little early."

"I'm . . . sorry for that. It's just that I had some things to think about. I might be taking a leave of absence . . ."

"Oh . . ." She looked at Fred, who stared at his shoes and bit his lower lip.

"Something wrong?"

"No," she said. "It's just that you're so easy to work for. I'd hate to think of someone bossy coming in here to take over."

"I . . . uh, don't foresee that happening, Ursula. It will only be for a couple of weeks, anyway. You are both perfectly capable of running things while I'm gone." He made his way to the door in halting strides, then turned.

They were watching him. "Thank you, Doctor." Fred grinned, rocking on his heels and bouncing on his toes. Those were the admiral's actions, and Fred had them down well. Did he imitate Irving Gushman too? Did he flummox the Gooshie words, pop open those Gooshie eyes, get all the idiosyncrasies perfect for the great amusement of Ursula and everyone else? It didn't matter. Not a whole lot did. Now.

"Does Admiral Calavicci know?" Ursula asked.

''Huh? Uh, no. I'm . . . I'm going to talk to him now.''

The pair giggled. ''I think he's still with Tina.'' Ursula's voice was barely a whisper.

''Still?''

''At least that's the word at the commissary,'' she replied.

Gooshie's earlobes burned. He stroked his mustache and looked away, wishing the mention of the admiral's paramour didn't inspire such a . . . heated reaction in himself.

''Well, I'll, um, just wait for him in his office, then.'' He stepped into the corridor, dug his hands into his lab-coat pockets and waited for the door to whisper shut. Only then did he allow himself to lean against the wall, shoulders slumping as his breaths rattled in his chest. So this was true *agita.* This is what it was like. He shook his head and pressed his lips together. *Welcome to the real world, Gushman.*

CHAPTER SIX

''Afraid?'' This was not exactly the reply Sam had expected.

''You would deny this?''

''I'm not afraid.'' He attempted a chuckle, which came out sounding more like a hacking cough. ''What could I possibly be afraid of?''

''God give me strength.'' Gerda's eyes rolled toward the ceiling, then back at him. ''I know you, Noah. Who do you think you're talking to here, Marilyn?''

''I—''

''Some wife she was,'' Gerda muttered. ''Never washed your clothes. You walked around looking like some bum off the street. I should get struck by lightning for pampering you so much, leaving you a helpless fool in her hands."

Okay, here we go.

"She hardly ever cooked for you, and when she did, the stuff was nearly inedible. I remember her specialty. Marilyn's Magnificent Meatloaf. Could have used it as a foundation brick."

Like your kugel, Mom? He wouldn't say it, wouldn't even hint at it. Noah was in enough hot water already.

"Marilyn Stein-Ellman. The Professional Woman. Pah!"

"*You* wanted a career, Mom," he couldn't resist pointing out.

She wagged a finger at him. "I still knew my place when it came to taking care of my husband."

"Your husband wasn't so great at taking care of you." Sam held his breath, waiting for the backlash that was sure to come.

It didn't.

Instead, Gerda grew pensive, pushing the rice around on her plate with her fork. "Your father was a very handsome man involved in a business filled with temptations. He was weak. I knew that when I married him."

"You don't have to make excuses for him." Had she always stuck up for Danny, even when he was making love to other women practically in front of her nose?

"I didn't go into that marriage with blinders on, Noah. I fell for him . . . hard. It was my own fault." Her shoulders slumped. "I paid for it."

"Are you bitter?"

Gerda cleared her throat, then took a long drink of water. She set the glass down gently and turned it round and round in the wet circle it had formed on the scratched tabletop. "When you love someone," she started slowly, as though the words were weighty and cumbersome, "you learn to overlook a lot. You of all people should know that, after four years of living with Marvelous Marilyn."

"Sometimes people marry too young," Sam said.

"Or they let the area below their waist do their thinking for them," Gerda added, without a trace of chagrin.

Cheeks burning, Sam made a great show of pulling off the lid of his soup bowl and digging into a wonton.

"You should have learned from my mistakes, but you didn't," Gerda said with a sigh, her eyes distant. She remained silent while Sam finished his soup. The quiet was as unnatural as a snowstorm in July, making him feel just as cold.

"What was I saying before you made me lose my train of thought?" she asked, as if waking from a dream.

Sam looked up from the dregs in his bowl. "Afraid. You said I was afraid. Of what I have no idea—"

Her chair's rear legs squealed against the linoleum as she pushed herself away from the table. Her eyes blazed, Sam's remark igniting a smoldering spark within them. A woman's anger alternately fascinated and frustrated him. It sometimes got his temper flaring to the point where the altercation became nothing more than a yelling match. But a loud verbal spar with Gerda would accomplish nothing except tears, and possibly a slammed door in his face. He had to be cool with her, had to let her ride with her anger.

"You're either afraid of taking a job where you won't be in charge," she spat, "or of working for a woman."

Sam raised his brows. "That's not true."

The salt and pepper shakers on the table rattled as she tramped over to the counter. She grabbed for the phone, but its wire was tangled in the paper towel holder over the sink. "Son of a bitch!" she yelled, wrenching the towel holder out of the plaster, nails and all, and hurling it into the sink.

"Mom . . . ?"

Teeth bared, eyes wide and focused on the task at hand, Gerda ripped a scrap of paper off the phone dial, then thrust the paper and the receiver at Sam. Her chest was heaving hard. "If you're so brave, prove it. Call her back, dammit."

For a moment, he could only gawk at her, feeling fortunate to have Leaped into her son and not a true antagonist.

"Call her. Go ahead, Mr. Courage."

The receiver was warm from her grip as he accepted it into his palm. He plucked the scrap paper from between her fingers, then brushed past her. As he did, he was surprised and heartened by a reassuring squeeze of his shoulder.

Sam dialed, stomach clenching as he realized he was about to accept a position he had no idea if he could handle. But every Leap was like diving head first into a new job—a job for which he was usually woefully underqualified. The prospect had long since ceased to frighten him—now it was simply a common, undeniable part of his world.

So why were his knees quaking so hard? The phone rang in his ear—once, twice. Al had said nothing about a Rebecca Wexler offering Noah Ellman a job. What was Noah qualified to do besides managing a music store? And would Sam Beckett be able to mold himself to fit whatever the job description required him to be? A few choice epithets for Ziggy popped into his head, as someone picked up . . .

"Hello?" The woman's tone was crisp, clear, like a silver bell. Sam tried to respond but his tongue felt caked with sand. He cleared his throat, panicking to find his voice.

"Hel-lo?" she repeated.

"M-miss Wexler?"

Silence. She was going to hang up, then he'd have to go through the embarrassment of calling her back, starting all over again.

"Yes?" There was a tightness in her voice, but at least she was still on the line.

Sam's shoulders sagged. Expelling a small breath of relief, he pressed on. "This is Noah. Uh . . . Noah Ellman."

"Oh . . . hello." The edge in her voice melted away. "It's so good to hear from you again. You know, I thought you were going to . . . leave me in the lurch here with this mess."

Mess? I'll be a janitor, maybe. Or a sanitation worker . . .

Sam raised a brow at Gerda, who looked at him hard.

"Mr. Ellman?"

"Uh . . . yes."

"You are calling to accept my offer, I hope."

"Yes . . . I'll take the job."

Gerda's grease-smeared smile could have brightened the inside of a chimney. He threw her a quick hesitant grin.

"I'm . . . so pleased." Rebecca let out a breathy laugh. Her relief seemed so strong. Was she clenching her stomach, waiting for her heartbeat to slow as the tension eased? Not one of Sam's six doctorates was in psychology, but by now he could have earned an honorary degree in it. That old familiar alarm sounded in the back of his mind. Its sibling was an anxious niggling in his entrails. He didn't need Al or Ziggy to tell him something was up.

"Our workday starts at nine, Mr. Ellman." Suddenly the voice was all business, almost brusque. "I need you to be here on time so I can show you what has to be done before my students arrive."

Students? Mess? A school custodian! Okay, no problem . . .

"I'll be there."

"Good . . ." She mumbled something unintelligible before her voice trailed off.

His immediate inclination was to ask if she was all right. Instead he murmured, "Good night, Ms. Wexler."

"You remember the address?" she asked.

"I . . . uh, think . . . I . . ."

She sighed, then recited it to him clearly and slowly, as if talking to a four-year-old.

"Got it!"

Softly, she said, "Good night, Mr. Ellman," and hung up.

Sam stared at the receiver, as if it could explain why that alarm clock buzz in his head was now a fire bell, why the niggling creature in his gut had sprouted pincers.

"*Nu?*" Gerda said, loading the empty food containers, bald rib bones, bits of plaster and nails and the demolished paper towel holder into a large plastic garbage bag.

"Yes, Mom. I start tomorrow." He placed the receiver gently back into its cradle.

"See? You went through all that hemming and hawing for nothing. Sometimes, you gotta admit that your mother is right, Noah."

"You were right, Mom."

"You got a job!" She threw her head back and gave a hoot of triumph.

"Yes I did."

"Now don't you feel good?"

"Definitely." *No, Mom,* he wanted to say. You *feel good, I feel like I'm teetering at the top of the first hill of a monster coaster. I've got about a hundred sickening drops and loops to look forward to before the ride ends.*

He grabbed a sponge off the sink and began wiping down the table, but Gerda's pop-eyed look of disbelief stopped him. "Don't try to butter me up so much, Noah. I already forgive you. Here." She shoved the garbage bag at him. "Take this to the Dumpster."

This time he found the doorway out of the apartment, and the Dumpster down the alley between Gerda's building and a bicycle repair shop. He allowed himself a self-congratulatory grunt and shoved the bag into the half-full container. He could imagine Al lambasting him: *Don't get cocky. You didn't even mention the talent show yet.* Sam chuckled. Al was always with him, playing at being his conscience, even when the imaging chamber wasn't on-line. *Get with it, kid. Remember why you're here.* "Yeah, yeah, yeah," Sam mumbled, traipsing back up the alley-way. *But maybe Gerda's not the only reason I'm here, Al,* he thought. *Maybe there's something else, some*one *else to consider.*

His shadow grew long in the yellow glow of the street lamp. He turned the corner, and could have sworn he heard Rebecca Wexler's nervous, relieved laughter flowing with the traffic and the cool autumn breeze.

CHAPTER SEVEN

How the morning started usually indicated how the rest of the day would go. Al found this to be true eighty-six point two percent of the time. A good morning put him in an agreeable mood for the ride into the afternoon and evening, even if there were a few fender benders along the way.

Judging by the way this particular morning had begun, he was certain nothing could sour his mood for the next twenty-four hours. When he returned from his visit with Sam, and after a quick peek in at Noah Ellman in the Waiting Room (the poor guy was wrapped in Sam Beckett's aura, all curled into himself like a snail), he went back to his quarters for a fresh cigar. There he found Tina, sprawled on his military standard bed, wearing a violet negligee, through which her most viable assets were revealed, and some new kind of heady musk, which sent his senses reeling. The effect of her early return from her mother's, and her titillating welcome, was that his body heeded her call without any further provocation.

A week in heaven would have paled in comparison to the ninety minutes Al had spent making love with Tina on the bed, on the carpet, in the shower and on the cold damp tile of the bathroom floor. And God, Time or Whoever had the decency not to throw any emergencies his way during their . . . meeting.

Tina. Al sighed her name like a lovesick schoolboy, strutting like a proud (satisfied) peacock toward the control room. He couldn't recall the last time their "rendezvous" had been so fervent. A little absence did make the heart grow fonder, he mused, still floating on the hazy edge of afterglow.

He arrived at the outer door of the control room, whistling a little tune. Cigar firmly planted between his teeth, he rocked on his heels and placed his palm against the black ID plate.

Silence slapped him in the face.

The corners of his mouth twitched down, his good mood faltering the minutest fraction. He slapped the plate in retaliation. Nothing happened.

What the hell . . . ?

"Good morning, Admiral." The silken voice of Ziggy greeted him from nowhere yet everywhere, lowering his mood another notch.

"Ziggy, what the hell is going—" Impatience grabbed him by the throat. He banged on the door, the cigar still clenched between his teeth. "Gooshie, open the damn door!"

"I'm afraid Dr. Gushman is not at his post."

''Where is he?'' Al yanked the cigar from his mouth and surveyed the deep teeth marks at the nub.

''Waiting outside your office.''

''Then who''—*bang!* his right fist slammed into the door—''the hell''—bang!—''is in there?'' Wincing, he clasped his hand to his chest, in a futile attempt to relieve the pain.

''Dr. Ursula Whitley and Dr. Frederick Hanover.''

''Why did Gooshie leave Frick and Frack in charge without telling me?'' He further assaulted the door by kicking it. ''Let me in there, Ziggy.''

''I don't believe you are in the best frame of mind to confront Drs. Whitley and Hanover. I believe your first priority is to confer with Dr. Gushman.''

Al grumbled, his gaze flitting in disbelief from the door to a spot on the glowing ceiling. ''Who's in charge here?''

''You are, Admiral.'' The walls glowed a soft shade of lilac.

''Don't pull that crap on me. Who taught you that color mumbo jumbo? Beeks?''

''Actually, Admiral, it was I who enlightened her to the calming effects of shade and hue. She is considering allowing me to do over the Waiting Room in this very color.''

The remnants of Al's afterglow were eaten up by his fury. He tramped down the hallway toward the elevator, the violet glow serving only to add fuel to his already flaming temper.

This wasn't a fender bender; it was a demolition wreck.

The ride up to the fifth floor and the subsequent walk past offices and conference rooms did nothing to ease Al's virulent state of mind. If anything, his rancor had heightened, as if a hot metal plate glowed white in the center of his gut. The walls were still that nauseating shade of violet. If he hadn't been so intent on thinking up some choice words for Gooshie, he would have ordered Ziggy to can it.

But when he turned the corner, what he saw turned his anger to shock, then concern. Head down, hands behind his back, Gooshie paced slowly outside the office door. He paused and looked up at Al's approach, his face a mask of dark intensity. Shadowy half moons cradled his eyes. His hair stuck up in unruly tufts, as though he'd pushed his fingers through it dozens of times. His lab coat, usually so pristine, was a mass of wrinkles and unidentifiable stains. Had he slept in it? Had he even slept at all? And he hadn't shaved! Gooshie hadn't shaved. Gooshie was adamant about keeping his face stubble free. Even during those difficult Leaps, when he had to pull an all-nighter, he would always manage to sneak off for a few minutes to wash and run a razor over his cheeks and chin.

Something was really wrong, and the realization made Al stutter-step to a halt. He was good at confrontations that involved a healthy argument, but ones involving emotional crises sent him hunting for Beeks. Al cleared his throat and ran a hand over his face. Gooshie was the one always on an even keel. No matter what problem came up, Gooshie never got flustered or cursed or lashed out . . .

The programmer resumed treading a path into the carpet.

Al opened his mouth to speak, but couldn't find the words. *Stop it!* he told himself. *This is Gooshie flustering you—Irving Gushman, the King of Halitosis!*

Straightening his shoulders, Al smoothed his red and gold shirt with the flat of his palms and gamely approached his programmer. But Gooshie didn't look up again until Al was close enough to smell what he'd eaten for an early morning snack.

"Phe-ew, Gooshie." Al wrinkled his nose and waved his

hand back and forth between them. "That's really rank, even for you."

Any other time, Gooshie would have laughed off Al's tactless remark about his breath. But now he merely stepped back, stone-faced, giving Al room to open the door.

As Al seated himself behind his desk, his first inclination was to lambast Gooshie for acting so . . . un-Gooshie-like. The admiral was not an unsympathetic man, but he had little tolerance for people who made major traumas out of small problems. Gooshie had no life outside of the project, so whatever was making him act like his world was caving in could probably be remedied inside of five minutes.

"What's going on, Gooshie?" Al asked, leaning forward, removing a fresh cigar from his shirt pocket.

"I need a two-week leave of absence."

The matter-of-factness of Gooshie's tone, the assured way he folded his hands in his lap, made Al's palms grow moist. This might not be such a small problem after all. Gooshie was out of his element anywhere but the control room. Usually he couldn't wait to get back to his keyboard. At staff meetings, his gaze would flit from the ceiling to the window, settling with great yearning on the door. Now he seemed calm and centered. Over the years, Al had developed a inner alarm system similar to Sam's. It was now yowling at full tilt in the back of his mind.

"You . . . you can't leave, Gooshie. I mean, who's gonna handle Ziggy when I'm with Sam?"

"I believe Drs. Whitley and Hanover are more than qualified to do the job, Admiral."

"I hate those whiz kids." He pouted and shook the cigar at Gooshie. "Besides, Ziggy won't stand for it."

"She'll have to."

"Since Sam left, she's had a hard time dealing with

loss.'' Now he was really going off the edge, trying to drum up sympathy for the hunk of nuts and bolts.

''She can cope for two weeks, Admiral.''

''Yeah? Tell her that.'' Al twirled the cigar between his fingers and gave Gooshie a hard look—a look that would usually have sent him cowering behind his keyboard. But this time, he returned that look and held Al's gaze until it was Al who looked away, breaking the standoff. He snapped the cigar into two flaking pieces and crushed them into his ashtray. ''Dammit, Gooshie, what the hell's the problem?''

''I need a two-week leave of absence.''

''Why?''

''It's personal, Admiral.''

Al wondered what personal business Gooshie could possibly have. He rarely left the complex, never received phone calls, except ones from his colleagues in other areas of the project. This was his life. This was it!

''I'd like to leave today.''

''What if . . . I don't grant you that leave?'' Al asked with a cocky abandon he didn't feel.

''Then I will be forced to hand in my resignation.''

''That's ridiculous, Gooshie.'' It was almost comical picturing the programmer, hat crushed on his head, suitcase in hand, waddling to the parking lot, settling himself into his ancient Honda Civic, then . . . gone in a cloud of hot desert dust.

''It's not to me.''

''Wanna talk about whatever it is that's making you so miserable?'' Al asked, keeping his annoyance in check.

Gooshie shook his head, then shifted his gaze toward the plush blue carpet.

''Maybe Beeks could help—''

''No!'' Gooshie shouted, his head jerking up.

His reaction reminded Al of Dolores DeLucks, a stripper whose supreme talents included bugging her eyes out in time with her posterior gyrations. Like Dolores, Gooshie's eyes looked as if they might drop out of his head with just an ounce more persuasion. Al decided he wouldn't let things go that far. He pinched a bit of the flaking cigar between his fingers, then let it drift down to the blotter. "Where . . . would you go?"

Gooshie blinked and shook his head. "I'd rather not say."

"What if there's an emergency? Or something."

"I think the Project can survive without me, Admiral."

"We . . . uh . . . we . . . need you here, Gooshie." There. It was as much groveling as Al was going to do.

"I won't be gone forever." He rose from his chair, then rested one arm on its leather back and looked at Al. "I'm very sorry about this."

"Not as much as I am. Ziggy's gonna throw a fit."

"I'll have a talk with her before I leave."

"Yeah. You know, come to think of it, that's a good idea, Gooshie. Why don't you do that now, then get outta here for a couple of weeks?" He dumped the demolished cigar into the wastebasket by the side of his desk. "I'll see you."

"Thank you, Admiral."

Al nodded and watched him go. When he heard the elevator door whoosh open and shut, he unlocked the lower left-hand drawer of his desk and removed the only item in it: a black plastic card. Only two of Quantum Leap's brass had access to the card: him and Sam's wife, the project director in proxy, Donna Alessi. Using the card in tandem with a sixteen-digit code, Al could open any door on the premises. Carefully, he selected three fresh Havanas from the wooden box on his desk, then lifted the box's false bottom. He removed a disc the size of a watch battery from the small compartment and tucked it into his shirt pocket along with the cigars. After securing the card in his left front trouser pocket, he exhaled slowly and headed for Irving Gushman's private quarters.

CHAPTER EIGHT

Sam liked Gerda Ellman's living room. The moment he sank into the sofa's faded, overstuffed cushions, he felt at home. Photos, memorabilia and knickknacks graced every available space. Wherever he looked, his eye was caught by something different, another unique souvenir of Gerda's life. Every picture, every item told a story.

One photo he was especially drawn to rested on a shelf above a tan armchair. It showed Gerda dressed in flapper garb—sparkly red dress with fringes at the hem, the same color hat embellished with pink feathers. Her expression was pure camp, eyes as round as two saucers, her mouth a cherry-red O, and she knelt slightly, her hands crossed over her knees. She was probably bringing down the house, doing the Charleston. A banner over her head proclaimed, WILDWOOD HOTEL TALENT SHOW—SUMMER 1948. Next to the photo was a trophy, a gold cup with a dancer on top.

Everything in the room was dust-free, immaculate. He pictured her taking each item off its shelf, lovingly polishing it, soaking in the memories it provided, then gently replacing it in its special spot.

To his left, next to the lamp on a dark wood end table, was a two-inch-high statuette of a silver horn. "Danny" was etched on its side. Beside it was a small black-and-white photo of a little boy, who proudly displayed the same prize. It had to be Noah, Sam thought. The room was filled with images of him as a boy, a teenager and a young man. In the picture with the horn, he wore a Wildwood Hotel T-shirt, his dark eyes gleaming with happiness and mischief. A masculine hand rested on his shoulder. Danny? If it was, the horn and the hand were the only concessions in this "memory room" to his ever having existed.

"Noah!" Gerda called from the kitchen. "Is it on yet?"

His gaze shifted toward the direction of the voice; he stewed for a moment—again having no idea what "it" was. Frustrated, his eyes swept the room's contents, as if one of the trophies, plaques or photos might jump up and give him a clue. A rectangular cabinet sat across from him. Nothing there. A cuckoo clock ticked brightly above it. "What does she mean?" he asked it.

"NO-ah." Gerda's slippers flip-flopped as she traipsed into the room. She wore a sky blue robe; her hair was wrapped in a towel fashioned into a lopsided turban. "It's almost time, for God's sake!"

"Gee, is it that late already?" He quirked her a small grin. "I had no id—"

"I cannot miss one minute of that show." Two impatient strides brought her in front of the cabinet. Bending slightly, she pulled open its double doors. "I know you think this is a waste of time, but it's very important to me." Inside was a twenty-one-inch TV on a slide-out shelf. Below it was a turntable and a receiver. Embedded into each door was a speaker. Gerda clicked on the television and twisted the dial to the proper station. "What time is it?"

Sam checked the cuckoo clock. "One minute after eight. Too bad the cuckoo didn't announce the hour."

"He never did. Your father bought that clock, so it's no surprise it doesn't work right. It's three minutes fast, lucky for you." She sat next to Sam, on the very edge of the cushion. Her hands fidgeted in her lap, eyes riveted to the TV screen as it came to life. The picture was fuzzy around the edges, its colors washed out, but at least the set worked. On the screen, a middle-aged man in a salmon pink leisure suit was hawking used cars. Gerda said slowly, "If you're going to compete, Noah, you have to know who came before you and what not to do."

" 'You Can Be a Star'?" Sam's jaw dropped as he pointed to the commercial. It was ending with Mr. Salmon Leisure Suit disappearing in a puff of smoke. "That's what's coming on?"

"Sssh!" As the brassy theme music blared, she dug her nails into his sleeve. Her tone was hushed, reverent, when she announced, "Here comes Gerard."

"Gerard—"

"Jerome. Gerard Jerome. Don't start, Noah. No matter what you think, that man holds a lot of sway with the judges. There he is. Ooh, Noah, in just four more nights me and Marty will be dancing for him."

Marty!

Gerard Jerome, the show's emcee, had a grin so bright, the glittering sequins on his jacket paled in comparison. His blond hair was swept up into a fifties-style pompadour, and his personal style was pure Vegas kitsch.

Gerda nearly swooned.

Sam wanted to know more about Marty. But asking her now would have been like sending her a phone call underwater. In her mind, she was in that television studio, preparing to play judge, jury and (possibly) executioner.

The acts came and went in quick succession, none escaping Gerda's scrutiny and criticism. Each performer or group was vying for the top spot in one particular category. Of these there were six, with three acts competing in each one: Make 'em Laugh, Emote!, Circus Time, Vocal Stylings, Terpsicory Splendor and Gerda's heat—Song and Dance. "To win top prize in your category is nothing to be sneezed at, for sure," she announced during a commercial break, "but I think Marty and me have what it takes to score the most points and take home the ten-thousand-dollar grand prize."

"Marty's pretty good, huh?" Sam asked with feigned nonchalance.

"He dances like a dream, Noah."

Her cheeks went beet red, leaving no doubt in Sam's mind that he'd struck a golden chord.

She added, "You never took the time to watch us rehearse or you'd know."

"I will—"

"Sssh, sssh, ssssh!" The show was back. It was time, according to Gerard Jerome, for Song and Dance.

"Now here, see?" Gerda shook a forefinger at the screen as the first couple glided onstage. "These two are so mismatched it's not funny. Part of their problem is the way they're dressed. A latin number like 'Tico, Tico' cries for bright clothes—reds, greens and golds. That black-and-white bodysuit does nothing for her, and what's he doing wearing pink leather? He looks like Porky Pig!''

Sam opened his mouth to comment, but she was off again.

''Why is he just weaving back and forth behind her while she's singing? His dance should paint a moving picture of the song. That's what Marty does while I sing the verse of 'Lullaby.' Here is a perfect opportunity for this joker to show his stuff and he's blowing it. And she should have sung this in a lower key; those high notes are killing her.''

Sam had to admit she was right on all counts. And this Marty must be quite good; Gerda was not easily impressed.

She was less vitriolic about the next two acts, deigning to throw a sprinkling of praise their way a couple of times. During the final commercial break, she predicted who the winners in each category would be, but choosing who would take the grand prize was tougher. The comedian with the bow tie had made her laugh so hard her sides still ached, but that ten-year-old boy dressed like Uncle Sam, who sang the patriotic medley, showed real promise. The judges liked to give the big prizes to youngsters, mainly, Gerda surmised, because it gave the show great press and made the audience go wild. Sometimes the judges were biased that way, but they wouldn't be once they saw Marty and her perform. ''We're gonna take their breath away.''

After the break, the winners were announced and Sam was not surprised to see that Gerda had chosen well. The ten-year-old took the grand prize, and most of the other contenders she picked won their categories. Porky in pink leather did not place at all.

As the credits rolled, Gerda crossed her arms and sat back with a self-satisfied smirk. She did have her finger on the pulse of the show. Sam had no doubts, even without having seen her perform, that she and Marty would take a top prize. But Marty had to show first.

''So is Marty as excited about the show as you are?''

''He just loves to dance. It doesn't matter where or who's watching.'' A small smile played on her lips, her gaze distant. ''He signed up for the tryouts for me.''

''That's nice.'' Sam nodded. ''Hey, I'd really like to wish him luck before the audition.''

She turned to give him a ''Mom'' look filled with suspicion. ''Noah, you couldn't have cared less about this 'dancing business,' as you called it, yesterday. I'm glad you've changed your tune, but now I'm worried. Are you sick, bubby, my pride-and-joy boy?'' She placed a cool hand on his brow, giving him an overblown look of concern. ''Should I call the ambulance?''

''No, Mom.'' Laughing, Sam removed her hand from his forehead and clasped it to his chest. ''Maybe you don't think so, but I worry about you. I mean, how do you know this man will even show up for the audition?''

''This is Marty we're talking about. He is the gentlest, kindest man I've ever met.'' Her fingers squeezed his tighter. ''He would never hurt me.''

Sam had a nagging feeling that Noah and Marty had never been formerly introduced. Playing hunches was a Leaper's forte, so he went with his. ''I want to know more about him. What's his last name?''

''NO-ah!'' Gerda released his hand, her eyes wide with disbelief.

''What is it?''

''Who's the parent here and who's the kid?''

''In this case that's irrevelent. We're both adults. You waited tables all those years, made sure I had enough to eat, decent clothes, and that we never had to spend the night shivering on a street corner. Now it's my turn to do some caring, and I want to know this guy's last name. Where is he from? What does he do when he's not with you?''

Gerda drew away from him. She brought one trembling hand to her cheek, then let it fall into her lap. Tears welled in her lower lids. "You never talked to me like this before."

"You pushed me into going for that job instead of letting me be lazy or throwing me out."

"Because I know that job is perfect for you. Rebecca is a vocal coach; you know music and you've done tons of paperwork in your career. Why do you think she wanted you so much?" She sniffed and fished a tissue from her pocket to dab at her eyes.

"Oooh, it's *Rebecca* now." Sam smiled.

"We had some wonderful conversations while you were going out of your way to avoid her. Did you know she had one hundred and fifty responses to her classified ad? One hundred and forty-nine other people would have grabbed that job, but she wanted you." She got off the sofa, shut the babbling TV, and grabbed a feather duster from behind the sofa.

"I'm flattered . . ." Inwardly, he sagged with relief. The job sounded interesting. And the best part was, it was something he could handle.

"You should be." The duster made a trip over framed photos, trinkets and shelves. The feathers just about grazed the items, and Sam thought this activity was just an excuse for Gerda to survey her things. "Ask her if she'll listen to me sing before the audition," Gerda said.

"Huh?"

With great care, she lifted a blue glass elephant off a shelf, then turned to Sam. "It wouldn't hurt for me to get some last-minute help. With her ear, she'll be able to tell me if I'm doing anything wrong. It'll give me an edge." She waved the duster at the empty spot on the shelf, then replaced the elephant.

Sam shook his head slowly. "I can't just ask this woman to listen to you for free. Vocal coaching is her livelihood. She's my new boss."

"She's also a decent person who really loves what she's doing. Believe me, Noah, she won't mind." After one final swing around the room, Gerda set the duster back in its place.

"I'll see how things go tomorrow."

"Sheesh, you're *still* afraid."

He raised one finger, about to reply, then realized she hadn't told him a thing about Marty. In her crafty way, she'd veered the conversation away from him.

"What about Marty?"

"What about him?"

"Full name, rank and serial number." He tried for a light tone, but didn't succeed.

"You're so on edge. Get some sleep." She dismissed Sam with a wave, and was almost out of the room when she turned on her toes to face him again. "Come to the rehearsal tomorrow night at the Starlight, if you really want to meet my Marty."

"I'll be there," he replied, but she was already gone.

CHAPTER NINE

"It's been a long time, Rebecca, hasn't it?"

"Yes."

"But here we are again."

"Yes."

"You thought it was over; you thought you were perfectly safe in your rooms, that you'd conquered . . . this."

The deep feminine voice came from over her right shoulder. It would be so simple just to turn and confront this nebulous presence but, as always, fear won out. If she looked into the woman's face, felt her breath against her cheeks, saw her mouth form each hateful word, something terrible would happen, something much worse than the horror that faced her now.

"One step, Rebecca."

"No." Her hands clenched, her nails digging deep into her palms.

"One step."

Rebecca moaned, letting her gaze drift over the idyllic shore. Here were warm sands, blue skies, clear waters lapping lazily at the sand. Two feet before her sat bowls laden high with pineapples and cherries, oranges and grapes. Her mouth watered. She could almost taste the tart sweetness of the fruit. This was supposed to be paradise.

But appearances could be deceiving.

"One step, Rebecca." The voice was coarser, more demanding now. The leaves on the trees behind her rustled fitfully at the sound of it.

"I . . . can't."

"You have no choice."

Those words were coming, those words that sometimes haunted her in waking moments because they were undeniably true. Rebecca struggled to put her hands over her ears, but she was not allowed. Her nails continued to gouge her palms. Warm blood dripped between her fingers, then made its languid way down to stain the bone white sand.

"You made your bed"—the woman's voice scraped like a monstrous talon against the walls of Rebecca's skull—"now lie in it!"

Sobbing, chest heaving, she took the one step, then another, feeling the familiar dread as the slow-motion horror began. The fruits exploded, splashing on her not the sticky pulp she expected, but blood. A rain of cherry pits flew at her face, her arms, every part of her. They clung to her, burning into her skin. Too many of them, she wanted to scream, but the blood was in her mouth now, trickling down her throat.

The ocean churned black; the sky was a terrifying mix

of violet and muddy green. The fluffy white clouds had transformed into hideous creatures with patent-leather skin. They drifted, grinning, red eyes gleaming. Their tails whipped the heavy air into a thunderous mass, sending down a rain of gold needles. With aching slowness, they assaulted her, each tiny tip penetrating a pore.

She could hardly draw breath, yet she was forced to take that one step, one step, one step . . . The shoreline beckoned. It was the only place left that didn't frighten her. It was her safe spot. Yes. Yes! Reaching it, finally, she sank to her knees, dug deep into the moist, cool sand and spread it over her face, her arms, her legs. It was a soothing balm, healing her wounds. Yes, here she was free from the horror, the pain. The monsters had gone from the sky, the blue was breaking through the violet-green. And the best part of all was that she was sinking. The sand was a cradle, rocking her, taking her gently into its depths. It claimed her lower extremities, then her torso. Now her ears, her eyes, her nose were almost gone. The sand filling her mouth tasted like pineapples and grapes.

And as the darkness ensued, elation gripped her. She was happy now, so happy because it was over . . .

"Momma!" She jerked upright, her heart beating so hard and fast she was sure it would drum a hole through her chest. *Deep breaths, count to ten.* Her eyes were still closed; her nails dug into her palms. *You're safe here, Rebecca. Feel the softness of your mattress? Breathe in the scent of the carnations you ordered from Haymer's yesterday. Remember? They're still fresh in the vase on your dresser.* She obeyed. The floral scent comforted her. *Now, lay your hands on top of the quilt you ordered from Macy's last winter.* The demanding yet sympathetic voice in her head wasn't anything like her own. Was it the same voice that tortured her on that sandy isle? She didn't know; she didn't want to think about it. Concentrating on its orders calmed her though. Her breaths hitched and slowed; her heartbeat went from a gallop to a trot.

The terror continued to abate by degrees as she brought her still-clenched hands from under the quilt and laid them on top of her chest. *Good, Rebecca, you're doing fine. Relax. Let your hands open.* This would take a while. It usually took an entire hour to regain her composure after the dream. It was back. The thought filled her with more dread than the nightmare itself. She thought she'd triumphed over it, setting up this very comfortable life for herself.

(You thought it was over . . .)

But this wasn't the case. It was with her all the time, lurking just below the surface, like some slimy aberration from the deep, waiting until she found confidence, satisfaction. Then . . . it pounced.

When she first made the decision (or when the decision was made for her) not to leave her house, the dream assaulted her almost every night. She cut her nails short then, since in her nightmarish terror they would gouge the tender skin of her palms. But recently she had regained the confidence to let her nails grow. Judging by the pain in her hands and the sticky wetness on her palms, she shouldn't have.

Now, if you open your eyes, you'll see you're in your safe spot, where you belong. Her safe spot. Letting out the breath she'd been holding for the past few moments, she made her eyes into slits. Everything was softness and shadows. She could pick out all the familiarities of the room without really defining them. Satisfied, she let her eyes close again. The clock ticking on her dresser lulled her. Outside in her backyard, a crow announced his arrival. She was back, safe and sound.

The terror had returned, Rebecca reasoned, because she

was inviting someone new into her life. As was true with so many other aspects of her existence, she didn't have a choice. Noah Ellman was necessary to her continued success and sanity. She refused to give in, call him and tell him not to come. Not after all the effort she'd made to convince him to work for her. The paradise flashed behind her lids, and the woman lurking over her right shoulder murmured something gruff and threatening in her ear. A chill ran down Rebecca's arms, but this time she refused to surrender. She kicked off her blankets, grabbed a wad of tissues from the box on her nightstand and dabbed at her oozing palms. Easing off the bed, she managed a few stumbling steps, then leaned against the post to survey her room. Her collection of biographies filled the shelves on her wall, her stereo stood next to them, waiting to offer her a Beethoven sonata or a Sondheim tune. The dresser she had owned since she was twelve was a comforting presence next to the window. The trunk filled with photo albums, sheet music and journals was still in the corner. Nothing could ever hurt again, not as long as she possessed all the pieces that added up to Rebecca. They constituted her impenetrable chain mail, and nothing, not even the subconscious part of her that rose up in the night, would ever completely break through it.

Satisfied that she had conquered the demons for another day, she allowed a small grin of triumph to touch her lips. It was time to scrub up, put on that fresh Rebecca face her students expected. Her stomach flip-flopped when she thought of Noah, but she quickly squashed the feeling. Noah was going to be a great asset to her. He would make sure her professional life was clutter-free. Her students would benefit by her newfound freedom, and everyone would be happy. Closing her eyes, she ran these thoughts through her mind like a mantra, until any trace of unease was gone. With renewed confidence, she opened her bedroom door and padded softly through the silent hallway to face the day.

CHAPTER TEN

Gooshie was gone. His Honda Civic had rattled him off into the sunset in a scene usually reserved for the hero not the coward. And a coward was what Al perceived the programmer to be. Heroes stay and face their problems. Cowards run.

The dust settled slowly around Al's red shoes. The shoes were the same color as his new Ferrari, which was why he bought them. In the past, he would never have worn them outside the project, not even to the parking lot to see someone off. But today Al's concerns ran deeper than getting a little desert dust on his ''Sunday-Go-to-Leaping'' attire. He had wanted to make very sure that when Gooshie bid him adieu, the suitcase with the tracking device inserted deep inside the fabric of its inner pocket went with him. Al had had no problem getting the device placed in the time it took Gooshie to have some lunch, make nice to Ziggy and leave Frick and Frack some last-minute instructions.

Now Gooshie could be tracked at least as far as the state line, and Al would bet the sticker price of his Ferrari that the programmer would go no farther than that. Gooshie was a homebody at heart. The Project was his home and hearth, and he would be loath to leave it too far behind. Once Al discovered where he was going, it might be easier to figure out what had caused him to take off in the first place.

Of course, the reasons for Gooshie's hiatus were not really anyone's business. But Al never let a little thing like a person's right to privacy stop him from getting to the bottom of a mystery.

Al crossed his arms, content that the first order of business of the day was done. In a few hours he would check the electronic surveillence kit in his room to see where Gooshie the gadabout had ended up. What he might do with that information he couldn't begin to guess. But he would cross that bridge when his red shoes brought him there. Turning on his new heels, Al tipped his scarlet fedora to the security guard at the lot's entrance gate, then headed back into the cool depths of the Project.

Sam Beckett had never had to sit at the kitchen table on a Sunday afternoon with the classifieds section of the paper spread out before him. Never had he had to wield a number two pencil, circling job openings for which he was somewhat qualified. In Sam's former world, jobs, scholarships and grants chased him. Job hunting, he was certain, was not a difficult pursuit in itself. Mind-numbing, perhaps. But the first day on the job—that was an intimidating prospect.

He recalled someone telling him once (Al, maybe?) that

geniuses might be able to get you to the stars but just ask one of 'em to make a decent slice of toast. Sam never had a problem when it came to dealing with the simpler aspects of life; perhaps it was because he grew up on a farm in Indiana. Slopping pigs and milking cows had never stunted his intellectual growth. Every morning he made sure he was up before the sun to do those chores. The routine helped him keep his feet firmly planted on the ground. So the first day on a new job would be equally as simple to deal with, right? He had devised a machine that moved him through time. He could handle this, couldn't he? In the mirror, the aura of Noah's hand trembled as it brought the razor just shy of his stubble. Sam froze, then set the razor on the edge of the sink, taking a deep breath to calm his quaking nerves. He didn't think he'd ever been this nervous, not even when he took that first step into the Accelerator chamber.

At five-thirty he had jolted awake, thirty minutes before the alarm was set to go off. The next few minutes were spent rifling through Noah's wardrobe for something suitable to wear. Pretty slim pickings, Sam thought, glowering at the flannel shirts and faded jeans in the closet. He was about to give up and start going through the dresser drawers, when he found a mint green dress shirt and a pair of charcoal-colored trousers, way in the back of the closet. He pulled them out, then laid them on the bed for a better look. The combination wasn't the greatest, but Noah wasn't Mr. *GQ* anyway. The outfit would have to do.

Now he was in the bathroom, studying the face he'd so far only seen in glimpses. Not a bad-looking guy, he thought, his composure setting in again—olive complected, straight nose, what a woman might think of as generous lips. He looked like some actor. He crimped his eyes and his image squinted back at him. He could have been one of those suave Mafioso guys, the type who's too charming and bright to get caught with the goods. With an arrogant tilt of his head, he tried out a somewhat seductive grin that came off looking more like a sneer. He lifted the razor again, this time with a steadier hand . . .

"Al Pacino!"

The razor slipped, nicking Sam's chin. "Al!"

"That's who you look like." The hologram stepped into Sam's peripheral view. "It's been bugging me since last night. Yeah, around the eyes and the mouth, and the way your hair's kind of hanging over your brow like that. You don't look as much like him as you did like Bogie that time you were the private detective. Remember that, Sam?"

"No," he grumbled, then heaved a frustrated sigh, watching a trickle of blood make its way down his neck. He let the razor clatter into the sink, grabbed a tissue from the box on the toilet tank and daubed the gash. "Why'd you sneak up on me like that?"

"I couldn't resist. It was the perfect situation: you making goo-goo eyes at yourself; I don't reflect. Hey, don't look at me like that. You'd do the same thing." He twiddled his eyebrows and retrieved the handlink from his jacket's inner pocket. "If you could."

"Thanks. Thanks very much." Sam stuck a swatch of tissue on the wound, then shaved around it the best he could. "I don't need this on the first day of Noah's new job."

"You got a job?" Al's fingers flew over the keypad. "How the hell did you do that overnight?"

Sam ran down the story in the time it took to finish his shave.

"Yeah, well, Ziggy's got nothing on Noah taking this job in the original history," Al said, checking the link. "He worked nights in a gas station on Kings Highway for ten years. When the station closed, he went on unemployment for six months before finding a job as a night clerk in a convenience store in Queens."

"I don't understand, Al." Sam leaned against the sink. "Why would someone with managerial experience seek out menial jobs paying minimum wage?"

"Who knows? Lack of confidence, lack of ambition, laziness. It can happen, but this is not why you're here. Gerda is, so don't start veering off course."

"Speaking of which," Sam said, "I found out her dancing partner's name." He faced the mirror again and ran a brush through the image of Noah's dark brown hair. "It's Marty."

"Marty . . ." Al prodded the link for a clue. "Uh-uh, Sam. Ziggy's got nada. Get a last name."

"I will but, you know, Al, this could be only part of why I'm here." Sam's voice was quiet.

"No."

"There could be another reason too."

"I don't like that 'I'm gonna save the whole damn world' look. Your eyes are all misty and you've got that dreamy smirk on your face. Aw, Sam. No!"

"Have Ziggy check out Rebecca Wexler."

"Who?"

"She's my b—"

"NO-ah, I have BA-gels." Gerda's call melded with the squawks of the handlink. "Come on. They're hot and fresh."

Al looked up and drifted toward the door. "That's Gerda, huh?" He poked his head through the wood and chuckled. "Nice hair."

Rolling his eyes, Sam set the brush down and sighed. "Al, could you just please do what I ask?"

"Noah, stop having a conversation with yourself and get in here."

"Re-bec-ca Wex-ler," Sam muttered through clenched teeth.

"Yeah, Sam." Al's lips twisted into a sly grin as he poked at the keypad. "You better do what Mom says. You don't wanna be late for work."

CHAPTER ELEVEN

Gerda bought the bagels using the change from the Chinese food. It was a special day, she announced, and a day like this should start out right. With a grand sweep of her arm, she set a toasted poppy-seed bagel before Sam as if it were a plate of eggs Benedict. A glass filled with water stood next to it.

"You look nice, honey." Gerda leaned against the sink, popping small pieces of onion bagel into her mouth. "But that shirt is so old. Why don't you wear one of the newer ones in the hall closet?"

Sam looked down and brushed a crumb off his tie. "This one's fine, Mom."

Al stood next to her, his eyes following her movements

as she ate. "She cares a lot about you. A guy should appreciate a mom who cares."

Sam stopped chewing as a memory blossomed. Al, his hair darker, his paunch not quite as prominent, was hugging Thelma Beckett. They were in the kitchen of Sam's sister's house in Hawaii. It was after dinner on some holiday—Christmas, Fourth of July, that part of the memory refused to surface. But tears were falling from Al's eyes. Sam remembered watching, almost mesmerized, as they slid down his friend's cheek to dampen the lacy collar of Sam's mother's blouse. Al never cried. He got angry, depressed, frustrated, but that time in Hawaii was the first time Sam had ever seen his friend get so emotional over his past. Al had revealed all about the dysfunctional Calavicci brood that day—how his mother ran off with an encyclopedia salesman, leaving him, his mentally handicapped sister, Trudy, and their father to fend for themselves. When his dad succumbed to cancer, Al was shunted off to an orphanage, and his sister to a mental hospital, where she eventually died.

"You don't know how lucky you are," Al said to him that day on the porch, his eyes red, his voice gravelly and thick. "Don't you even think of taking what you have for granted."

"Noah?" Gerda was shaking him. Quickly he swallowed what remained of the half-chewed bagel in his mouth and washed it down with the tepid water.

"Earth to Sam." Al hitched up a brow. "Why don't you ask her about Marty again before you leave?"

"Uh . . . yeah. Mom?"

"Honey, are you okay? You're not nervous, are you?"

"Well," Sam shrugged, "maybe a little."

"Listen to me." She pulled up a chair and sat beside him, clasping his hands in hers. "A long, long time ago, before I went onstage for the first time at the Wildwood, I was so petrified, I threw up all over Natalie Berchmyer's yellow pumps. That was in the dressing room. I had to redo my makeup and give her the ten dollars for new shoes. But you know what?''

''She went out there and knocked 'em dead,'' Al said.

''You floored 'em.'' Sam touched her cheek.

''You know it, baby. And after you get settled into your new job, Miss Wexler will wonder how she ever got along without you.''

''Mom?''

''Yeah?''

''Tell me about Marty.''

At the mention of his name, her face lit up, eyes shimmering like a pair of dark jewels.

''Boy, she's got it bad, Sam,'' Al said.

''He's a wonderful man.'' She set her elbows on the table, leaning her chin on her hands. ''When you talk to him he really listens. Not like some men who just hear what they want to hear . . .''

Sam gave Al a look.

''Last name, Sam.''

''That's great, Mom. That's wonderful, but what about him? What do you know about him? Is he married?''

Gerda hooted. ''Marty married? Good lord, Noah, the man's too wrapped up in his work to even think about that.''

''What does he do?''

''He's in school right now. NYU. Marty is very bright.'' She floated back to earth, her eyes searching Sam's. ''Since when are you so interested? I had all I could do to make you sit still when I told you about the audition.''

Sam tapped his fingers together. ''I just don't want to see you hurt.''

''Last name, Sam,'' Al said again.

''Marty's the last person who would ever hurt me.'' She checked her wristwatch and then the wall clock. ''You'd better go if you expect to get to work on time.'' She pushed away from the table and was about to take Sam's plate when his hand on her arm stopped her.

''What's Marty's last name?''

Her brow furrowed, her mouth twisted with annoyance. ''What's this all about? Are you going to check him out with the FBI?''

''Please?''

She pulled away and brought Sam's crumb-laden plate to the sink. ''It's on the show's application form.''

''Good, let's see it.'' Sam held out his hand.

''I can't get it now, Noah. It's in the safe deposit box in the bank. I'll try to remember to go for it later.''

''I can get it,'' Sam said. ''Just give me the key.''

''Sa-am, she's not gonna let you—''

Hands on hips, Gerda gave him a stern look. ''Noah, I want you to calm down. You will meet Marty tonight at the rehearsal. Then you'll see he's all I said he is.'' She pulled Sam's arm so hard he nearly tipped out of his chair. ''Now, get out of here. Go to work.''

Smoothing his shirt, he shuffled out of the kitchen to the sound of Al chuckling.

''And don't forget to ask your boss if she'll listen to me sing,'' she called after Sam as he stepped out the door.

Officially it was autumn, but the air held none of its chill. It felt more like early July, with just a hint of a breeze eclipsing the heat. As Sam walked to the corner, a light sheen of perspiration formed on his brow. He wiped it on his sleeve, waiting for Al to get directions to Rebecca's house from Ziggy.

"You're in luck, Sam. She's only four blocks west from here. You can hoof it."

Slinging Noah's windbreaker over his shoulder, Sam fell ino step next to the hologram.

"You think Gerda will keep her word?" he asked.

"I don't know, Sam. She seems awfully preoccupied." Al rattled the handlink, then clapped its side with the palm of his hand. "If she doesn't get you his last name, you'll have to ask him for it."

"Oh, sure. I'll just waltz over to him in the ballroom and—"

"Hey, Sam, that's a good one." Al hooted. " 'Waltz over in the ballroom—' "

"—ask him for his name. What am I, the dance-hall police?"

"Sam, you're pretty good at wheedling information out of people. I have great confidence in you." He throttled the link again; it screeched as if its innards were being scorched.

"What are you battling with Ziggy over now?" As much data and theoretical hypotheses as the hybrid computer was able to impart, she was never one to give them up without a squawk. Sam figured jamming up the handlink was simply her way of proving her superiority—her way of saying *You need me more than I need you.*

"There!"

"What?"

"I wanted to get you the lowdown on Rebecca before you met her." His eyes grazed the link appreciatively. "She's made quite a name for herself in this town. Some of her 'kids' as she calls them have gone on to star in a bunch of the biggest shows on Broadway; others have done commercials and movies. Ninety-five percent of her students have had some measure of success in the entertainment industry."

"Yeah?" Sam strained to see the green letters scrolling across the screen.

"*New York* magazine did a feature on her a few months back called 'The Entertainment Industry's Best Kept Secret Is Living In Brooklyn.' "

"I wish I knew why she sounded so strange on the phone . . ."

Al looked up from the link. "Uh-oh."

"What?"

"Here we go again. Why do you keep trying to veer off this very simple course? Gerda is the one who is in danger. Ziggy gives it an eighty-nine point two percent chance of being why you're here. Rebecca's still alive in our time, still living in the same house as a matter of fact—"

The link howled like a banshee, then died at the same time a jabbering group of teenaged girls passed through the Observer.

Sam stopped in his tracks and glowered. "What's going on, Al?"

"Hmm?" Al was torn between restoring Ziggy's services and admiring the sweet young things disappearing down the street.

"What's wrong with Ziggy?"

"You're gonna be late—"

"Tell me."

An elderly couple strolled by, giving Sam a half-apprehensive, half-sympathetic look.

Al squirmed and shook the link. Its lights flickered; it mewed like a sick cat. "She's in a bad mood."

Sam grumbled. Dragging information about the project out of Al was like trying to entice a kid out of Disneyland. He sometimes wished Al would ignore the rules, rules Sam had set down before he Leaped, and really give him the lowdown on things. Quantum Leap was Sam's creation. At one time it was Sam Beckett who held the final word about what went on there. Now he was relegated to being spoon-fed bits and pieces of information when Al slipped up, or Ziggy started acting weird, like now. True, Al didn't want to give him any more to worry about. But sometimes Sam really wanted to be more involved, to know that on some level the control of his life's work hadn't been completely handed over to others.

"Why is she in a bad mood?"

Al rolled his eyes and kicked at the ground. "Because Gooshie went away for a couple of weeks."

"So he went on vacation. What's the problem?"

"Sam." Al met his eyes. "The last time Gooshie took vacation was because I forced him to go. He hadn't left the complex in two years. Ziggy was informed way in advance. She was no barrel of laughs then but she wasn't this bad."

"And now?"

"Gooshie just left. Threatened to quit if I gave him a hard time." He tapped his foot, gazing at a spot just over Sam's right shoulder. "That's the first damn time he got up enough chutzpah to talk up to me. Pffft. He was gone! Wouldn't tell me why or where. I'm tracking him though."

Sam crossed his arms and shook his head in amazement. "You put a tracking device in his luggage."

"You know it."

Across the street someone was waving at him. Mary Jane Wax! She was standing at the bus stop, book in hand, pocketbook over her shoulder. *It's all right*, she mouthed, then pointed to her forehead and nodded, despite the morning passersby snickering and staring at Sam.

They walked the next couple of blocks in relative silence; occasionally Al's comments about Gooshie's newfound chutzpah would punctuate the quiet like exclamation points.

"Turn here, Sam."

They rounded the corner and it was almost as if they'd been transported to another town. No ancient apartment buildings with their faded bricks and rusted fire escapes lined these streets. No dried brown strands of grass struggled through cracks in these sidewalks. The houses here were old yet stately and well maintained. The lawns were manicured. Somehow, the eighty-degree heat was less oppressive here. Autumn was in the air. The trees, still green, seemed to be just waiting to turn to gold and red.

"She lives right here, Sam." Al led him to the second house from the corner. It wasn't as expansive as some of the other homes on the block. The wide porch was a simple affair with no columns or decorative overhanging eaves, possessing not even a swing or a wrought-iron bench. Over the doorway, wind chimes shaped like music notes and treble clefs tinkled gently in the warm breeze. Sam couldn't resist brushing them with his fingertips, enjoying their ring-tingling cacophony. On either side of the door were two large windows, both with their curtains closed. Beneath each window was a barren windowbox. Sam drew a forefinger across the edge of one, noticing a dead butterfly lying in the dust on the bottom.

"Go ahead."

Clearing his throat and straightening his shoulders, Sam knocked on the door.

"Just a minute," a feminine voice called from inside.

Sam took a step back as the curtain to the right of the door drew away just enough to reveal a blue eye peering out. In an instant the curtain fell back and the door clicked open a crack.

"I guess that's your greeting, Sam."

Affecting his most confident smile, Sam stepped inside the house.

CHAPTER TWELVE

There is so much to think about. Gerda's head was reeling. *Rehearsal tonight. Remember those beats before Marty's entrance. That's the trickiest part of the act. One, two, boom, boom, and step . . . step . . . right into his arms. And your dress—don't wear the black one tonight, that's the one for the audition. The red one will do—the one with the sequins.* She spread her arms wide and twirled three times in the middle of her bedroom. In her mind she was dancing beneath the three giant mirror balls that twirled over the Starlight Ballroom's dance floor. Marty was with her, of course. He was always with her in her fantasies. Together they traveled the country, hitting all the dance spots together—the nightclubs, the dive bars with sawdust on the floor and a jukebox blaring in the corner, even the discos. Sure, why not? They would stay over at cozy bed and breakfasts, instead of those impersonal eight-hundred-room hotels. She and Marty both enjoyed the simpler things in life. They'd discussed traveling, although obliquely. *Have you traveled the country much Marty? Nah, me neither. It's expensive, yeah. But I think if I could afford it, I would like to see every part of it . . .*

Gerda never allowed the conversation to get too personal; she would never think of letting Marty know how she really felt about him. He would run from her so fast his shoes would leave scorch marks down Flatbush Avenue. She was old enough to be his grandma, for God's sake, and here she was having these silly romantic notions about him, like he was Cary Grant or Fred Astaire.

Marty, oh, Marty. Your friend Gerda is such an old fool.

Marty. It wasn't even his name. She giggled, pulling a brush through her hair, wrinkling her nose with displeasure at the gray roots showing through. Her hairdresser's appointment wasn't for another hour yet. She had to get to the bank before then to cash her Social Security check, which had just come in the mail. But she still had a few minutes to dream and dance.

Marty. It was the name of the character Ernest Borgnine played in that movie of the same name. It had always been one of Gerda's favorite films, and when she met her Marty a few months back, standing forlorn and alone in the corner of the Starlight Ballroom, it immediately came to mind. The character in the movie was a lonely middle-aged butcher who thought, *Whatever it is women like, I ain't got it.* He was proven wrong when he eventually met his schoolteacher love. And though the plotline did not mirror her situation, and her Marty was only in his late twenties, she couldn't help finding similarities between the character and the man she knew.

He had laughed when she pinned him with that nom de plume. Now it was almost as if he *became* "Marty" when he was with her, leaving that other guy outside the ballroom doors.

What *was* that other guy's name, anyway? Noah wanted to know, didn't he? Gerda placed the brush on her bureau, then knelt to retrieve her sneakers from beneath the bed. She grabbed a couple of dust bunnies too and threw them in the wastebasket in the corner. Lately she had become remiss where household chores were concerned. Between worrying about the audition and pushing Noah to accept Rebecca's offer, her mind just wasn't on grabbing the mop and pail. After the audition, she promised herself, she would get back into the swing of things—especially if she were able to convince Marty to come over for dinner. So far he'd declined every one of her invitations, saying he had to study or visit his relatives or some other silly excuse. She didn't fall for any of it. The age gap was the roadblock, she knew. Why should a bright young man want to spend time off the dance floor with an elderly old coot like her?

But you're not an old coot. In the mirror a slim woman wearing a red tank top and jeans glared at her with defiance. "Yes, I am," she replied to her image. "He only continues to meet me at the Starlight because I can keep up with him on the dance floor. Most of those women there don't give a hoot for the cha-cha and the tango. Dancing is just an excuse for them to meet men." The woman in the mirror threw her head back and laughed. *And wasn't that your original motive?* "Maybe it was a long time ago. But you know that after a while I got sick of the hunt and just danced for the sake of dancing. That's when I met Marty." She smiled warmly at the memory and began humming

"Lullaby of Broadway," the song they would be using for the audition.

The alarm clock on the dresser caught her eye in the middle of the second verse, jolting her from her reverie. Ten thirty-five. She had been daydreaming much too long; now she barely had time to get to the bank before the hairdresser's appointment at eleven. She grabbed her pocketbook off the doorknob. After checking for her keys and her purse, she hurried out the door.

CHAPTER THIRTEEN

The first thing Sam noticed was the desk. It was, he thought with stomach-clenching certainty, all his. Papers, file folders and manila envelopes sat in ragged towers on top of it, waiting with infinite patience for someone (him!) to come along and put them in some sensible order.

The next thing he noticed was her. Arms crossed, she leaned against the arched entranceway to the rest of the house, staring at him, wearing a "cat that ate the canary" grin.

"Told you so," she said. Her look was a challenge, but he couldn't meet it. His eyes flitted to the beveled-edge wall mirror, to the upright piano in the corner, the plants hanging by the windows, by the doorway (but there were none in the windowbox), the ficus tree in the corner by the many-cushioned sofa, the music stands, the wall shelves filled with books, and finally to Al. The Observer's eyes were knowing, and no less amused than Rebecca's. Ignoring the pounding of his heart, Sam turned slowly to look at her again.

Something about her . . .

"Are you up for it, Noah?" she asked, approaching the desk.

"He's rarin' to go, kid." Al favored her with an appreciative once-over.

"It's . . . why I'm here."

Placing her hand on top of the middle pile of paperwork, she looked like an explorer claiming a piece of land. "I don't have much time to go over everything with you. My first student will be here in about"—she checked her watch—"oh, twenty minutes. Sit." She indicated a leather chair at the desk, nearly lost behind the sea of paperwork.

Sam sank into the chair's comfortable depths as she pulled over a wooden stool and sat beside him. "What you saw on the desk when you were here for the interview was just the tip of the iceberg. Most of this stuff is weeks old. I'm . . . way behind." A flicker of concern/worry/sadness put a hairline crack in her confident veneer. Yes, here was the woman Sam had spoken with last night.

"Just tell me what to do," Sam told her softly, "and it'll get done."

She cleared her throat and ran her hands through her honey blond hair.

. . . Something about her—a vulnerability, a melancholia, that had been obvious to him without even seeing her made him think, made him know *she was part of why he was here.*

"You're going to start with these applications right here." She tapped the pile directly in front of him. "These kids are the ones who've had some professional experience and now just need a little extra help. They would only need a few lessons, since their main problem is puberty—"

"I never considered that a problem." Al strutted through the desk, situating himself between Sam and Rebecca. He hitched a brow, seemingly nonplussed by Sam's warning glare.

"—rearing its head to mess up their vocal range. I can help them adapt. You'll need to refer to my schedule, which is in the middle drawer, and set up interviews wherever you see a free hour Monday through Saturday. That doesn't include lunch hour, which, as you will discover, is vital to my sanity." She fixed him with those blue eyes. To his dismay, he wondered how her flowing honey blond hair would feel entwined between his fingers, how the tiny cleft in her chin might feel caressed by his thumb. He coughed, then fumbled for the application on top of the stack, his face growing hot as he skimmed through it.

He never welcomed the first signs of a burgeoning attraction. Where could the relationship lead? His Leaping allowed him time only to savor the promise of something great then . . . leave the relationships to someone else's care. What if that someone else didn't want to finish what he'd started? He swallowed, guilt snaking through him, unwelcome. How many times had this happened over the course of his Leaping? He always tried his best not to allow his emotions to carry him away. But sometimes they did, assuaging his loneliness for a time. A flash of memory hit him: of a lingering kiss, a caress, a moment when his needs had taken priority. He smelled something light, floral. Re-

becca's hair brushed his hand as she bent to see what he was looking at . . .

"It's all pretty simple—name, phone number, professional experiences and goals. If the kid is under eighteen, always talk to the parent first."

"What . . . about the rest?" Sam waved his hand across the other two uneven towers.

"Those are the ones who'd have to sign up for a longer term with me, if I took them on. I'm going to have to weed out the ones who don't have what it takes." A pained look crossed her pale face. She rubbed her forehead. "We'll deal with those later in the week. I just wanted you to see what you were getting yourself into." She perked up suddenly, smirking like a mischievous ten-year-old as she looked hard at his face. "Did anyone ever tell you you kind of look like Al Pacino?"

"Yeah. Just around the eyes and the nose." He smiled at Al, who was bobbing on his toes, sporting an "I told you so" grin.

The handlink bleated like a sheep at the slaughter. Al's face darkened. He lifted one fist to strike the link, but lowered it slowly after a moment, flapping his lips in frustration. "I'd better go help Frick and Frack deal with Miss Temperamental." After he tapped in the proper code, the imaging chamber portal whooshed open behind him. Sam waited for a parting remark about Rebecca's attributes, possibly a "Have fun, you two." But it was not forthcoming. Al's face was a mask of worry as he stepped back into the light and vanished into the future.

There was a knock at the door. Sam lowered his eyes to immerse himself in the application in his hands until another, more insistent knock sounded. He gave Rebecca a questioning look and she responded by waving her hand toward the door. "Another facet of your job description, which will grow as long as you are employed here, is that you, Noah Ellman, are my official doorman."

She didn't like to answer the door, he thought, returning the application to the top of the heap and pushing away from the desk. She didn't like plants in her window boxes, but she loved them around her house. The alarm that had been burring softly in the back of his mind since he arrived grew a few notches louder. He opened the door, letting in a teenaged boy with slicked-back hair and a poor attempt at a mustache. Beneath one arm he carried a worn leather pouch. Sheets of music paper stuck out of its opening, their edges frayed and bent.

"I was just kidding about the doorman thing, Noah," she said. "Leave the door unlocked. The kids are used to just walking in."

"Mornin', Ms. Wexler." The boy tossed his pouch on her sofa.

She gave him a stern look, which caused him to immediately retrieve his papers and hand them to her. "Sorry," he mumbled.

"This isn't a place to flop, Ralph, it's a place to work. You've got to be prepared mentally when you arrive or we'll never get anything done." She met Sam's eyes. He was still holding the door open, admiring how well she handled her charge. "And there is a great deal of work to be done, isn't there, *Mr.* Ellman?"

Ralph cringed and looked down at his shoes as Sam let go of the door. It hissed shut as Sam hurried back to his desk. He focused on the papers. Rebecca was kidding with Ralph now, putting him at ease. Her voice was as lilting as the sounds that must fill the room when she sang. Sam peeked over the middle pile of papers, noticing how the melancholia in her eyes didn't fade even when she smiled. Gerda's dilemma haunted him too. But he relegated this and his other problems to some distant corner of his mind. Discipline, he thought, settling into his chair and delving into the mountain of work. It was the only thing that would get him through this day.

CHAPTER FOURTEEN

Frick and Frack were not happy campers. Al could sense their tension and frustration as he tramped down the ramp leading from the imaging chamber. Seated side by side behind the console, heads bent, they were completely immersed in their work. In contrast, the gorgeous pulsating rainbow emanating from the orb on the wall frolicked over them, the console, the floors and the walls as if it were playtime. The orb was the heart and soul of Ziggy, the colors a reminder that she held sway. And the brilliance of those colors meant she was not a happy camper either.

Ursula raised her head. Her brown eyes, usually bright and impish, were now heavy-lidded and somber. "We're having some problems with the monitors, Admiral."

"What . . . kind of problems?" He made his way around to Ursula's work area. A hodgepodge of disturbing images played on her screen: a horde of unruly protesters being beaten by riot police in front of the White House, a picket line moving with zombie-like slowness in front of a car-manufacturing plant, a variety of advertisements zipping by so fast Al could only pick out the slogans—"Strike it rich!," "Lucky Strike," "You gotta strike while the iron is hot." In each ad, the word "strike" lingered a millisecond longer than the others. Occasionally the data screen would pop into view, but was replaced after twenty or thirty seconds by the crazy-quilt imagery.

"Dammit." Al gritted his teeth, Ziggy's message hitting him with the force of a Mack truck. Glaring at the orb, Al pulled a cigar from his jacket pocket and twirled it between his fingers. "Don't do this, Ziggy."

"I don't know how we can get any work done if she keeps this up." Fred placed his fists on either side of his keyboard, his frown deepening.

A vein ticked over Al's right eye. "Looks like Ziggy's gone on strike."

Fred's jaw dropped and Ursula scrunched her eyes at him, causing Al to wonder if he'd sprouted another head.

A close-up of a bearded man wearing a bandana and a nose ring appeared on the screen. He opened his mouth wide enough so that his back teeth were visible, shouting, "Stri-i-i-ke!"

The years had mellowed Al. When he was active in the military, the least bit of insubordination from anyone would send him into a tirade. Warnings from his doctors, plus years of observing life alongside Sam Beckett, had made him more tolerant. But not when it came to a certain hybrid computer.

"Ziggy!"

"I can hear you, Admiral." The computer's tone was as sharp as the hues she was projecting. "There is no reason to shout."

Frick and Frack were staring at him, their eyes glassy with exhaustion. They were just waiting for him to lose it, he could tell. What great conversation that would make in the commissary.

"I'm going to my office, Ziggy." He chomped the unlit cigar between his teeth. "We gotta talk."

"What the hell do you mean disrupting the whole project with your stupid, egocentric antics?" The admiral stood in the center of his office, between his desk and a bookcase, staring daggers at an indiscriminate spot on the ceiling. He had no idea why he always looked heavenward when he spoke to Ziggy; looking down would have made a lot more sense.

"The concept of striking intrigues me," she said. "I used to wonder why humans went through such trouble making their demands known." She seemed to pause for effect, which was not something Sam had programmed her to do. She was acquiring more humanlike qualities all the time. "Now I know."

"Ziggy, one of your oars is not in the boat."

She ignored his comment. "Striking calls for desperate measures. It seems, Admiral, the more management is inconvenienced, the more quickly the striker's demands are met."

If he ever wanted to take the wire cutters to her innards, it was now. "Ziggy, Gooshie left on his own accord. He will be back."

"I want him back now."

"He went on vacation once—"

"He prepared me for that eventuality in advance. I do

not take well to sudden changes in my routine.''

''It's only for two weeks! Anyway,'' he continued with offhanded ease, ''he didn't tell me where he was going.''

''You put a tracking device in his suitcase, Admiral. Did you forget? Hmmmm?''

Al shrugged, wondering how he could have even attempted to put one over on her. ''All right, let's negotiate.'' The idea pained him, but it was the only way he was going to keep the peace.

''We need a mediator. There is generally an unbiased party present to—''

''No!'' Al paced the length of the room, from the wall to the door. ''Here's my offer, and you'd better damn well accept it. You will cease and desist projecting strike scenes on the control room's computer monitors while Sam and I figure out who this Marty guy is. Seeing as how you can't.'' He paused to let the dig sink in. ''When that's done, I'll get in touch with Gooshie and express your disappointment over his actions.'' Silence was the only reply, causing Al's temper to flare. He kicked the side of his desk, shouting, ''Dammit, Ziggy, answer me.''

''I will consider your offer and get back to you in twelve point seven hours.''

''Ziggy, you're working against yourself. You're not being logical.''

''It's all part of the strike strategy.''

''Your main priority is Sam.''

''I would not keep you from contacting him, Admiral. I just need to inconvenience you. A striker needs to communicate her message in a way that will make everyone sit up and take notice.''

Al flopped down on the edge of his bed and scrubbed his hands through his hair. ''We've noticed. We're inconvenienced. Happy?''

Her silence was riling him again. Before he could lose his temper, he got up and went to the door. Maybe Tina could jammer some of Ziggy's bolts and chips and force her to stop. But how would Ziggy react? Would she use some backup program to intensify her "striking strategies," gumming up the works even more. No. His shoulders slumped. It wasn't worth the attempt.

"Oh, by the way, Admiral, I thought I might correct one of your earlier comments."

His hand froze inches from the ID plate near the door. "What?"

"The strike images are not being transmitted exclusively to the control room monitors anymore."

Al breathed a few choice words he once overheard in an enlisted men's latrine.

"I have now decided to transmit them to every monitor in the complex."

CHAPTER FIFTEEN

If someone had told him there would be a spring in his step as he headed back to Gerda's apartment, Sam wouldn't have believed it. But here he was, whistling, almost dancing, down the sidewalk.

The work had been engrossing, if not challenging. He set up over two dozen appointments and left five or six messages. Still he hadn't gotten halfway through the monstrous pile. That was okay. He was actually looking forward to plowing through more of the same tomorrow. The front room was large enough so that sounds carrying over from Rebecca's work area were in no way intrusive. The music was a welcome perk. Rebecca's students were young, yet so devoted to their craft it was as if they had been born with the need and drive to succeed. Their repertoires were diverse. One little girl with Shirley Temple ringlets belted out the Rolling Stones's "Get Off My Cloud" and after that a Puccini aria. No matter what the student's forte, Rebecca made sure he or she sampled from each plate on the musical smorgasboard. Her motto was that it was "all music." She exalted the raw grittiness of the blues, the uplifting message of gospel, the plaintive yearning of country and western. To prejudice yourself against any type of music, she said, was like not reading a particular novel because its cover was the wrong shade of yellow. Her analogies were innovative and humorous, and never failed to win her a laugh.

Rebecca was a hard taskmaster, but the kids respected her, basking in her praise, taking her criticisms and suggestions and utilizing them to improve. She had a way of making each one feel special. And no one ever left her lesson without a grin plastered across his or her face.

Sam turned the corner, stumbling out of the way of a little boy on a trike. A wave of vertigo hit him and he leaned against a lamppost, taking deep breaths until his legs felt sturdier. His stomach rumbled, reminding him he hadn't eaten at all that day. Gerda had bought bagels with the money he might have taken to buy lunch, but that was okay too. Lunchtime had been spent strolling around the block a few times, the melodies of the morning playing in his head like a movie soundtrack. He recalled the intense look on Rebecca's face as she listened to her students. At times she'd let one hand drift up and down like a leaf on a gentle wave, illustrating how she wanted to hear a certain phrase sung. Sam had to push himself to concentrate on his work, so entranced was he by her.

The music chased off her demons, but at the end of the day they returned. Sam could tell by the way Rebecca's hand trembled slightly as he shook it in farewell. Her eyes were bright with excitement, but there was a wisp of fear in them. She did not look forward to being alone. Two spots of color appeared high on her very white cheeks. He almost asked if she'd like to join him for dinner, but he had no money. Plus, he reminded himself, he had to go to Gerda's rehearsal to meet Marty.

It could all be over tomorrow. Tonight he would dig for the information he needed to figure out why Marty had originally reneged on his promise. If it was because of an accident, Sam would be try to steer him away from the danger in time. If it was something else, something that made him run, Sam would find that out too, and work to remedy the problem. He had to make Gerda his priority. The sudden, unbidden memory of Rebecca's soprano as she harmonized with Ralph on *West Side Story*'s "Somewhere" made him catch his breath. *It could all be over tomorrow.*

He did an old man's shuffle down the block, in case the sidewalk decided to tilt again, and eventually made it to Gerda's building. Closing his eyes, he heaved a grateful sigh, leaning back against the cool bricks, clenching and unclenching his fists. Just once he would like to not feel guilty about his desires. There must have been times when he hadn't, when he had refused to worry about the consequences of just . . . giving in. He lifted his head and turned to look at the twilight settling over the buildings. Lights burned in windows. It was dinnertime. Gerda would have a plate set for him, he was sure. She was a good mom, as Al had said. Don't take anyone who cares for granted.

Scrubbing a spot of moisture from his cheek, he pushed away from the wall and tramped up the stairs to his home.

As he stepped into the apartment, the aroma of roast chicken caused his hunger to override his self-pity. In the kitchen it waited for him, steaming and golden on his dinner plate. The rumbling in his stomach could have shaken the building to its foundations. He washed up in the kitchen sink and could hear Gerda singing in the next room. From the thump, thump of heels on the carpet, he surmised she was practicing her dance steps as well.

Ravenous, he dug into the chicken, mashed potatoes and string beans, giving silent thanks that the dinner was a major improvement over the kugel of the night before.

''Noah, oh, Noah.'' Gerda shimmied into the room, primping at her hair. She was a vision in red sequins, her face rouged, eyelashes thick with mascara, her lipstick matching her flame red hair. ''I'm so glad you're here. Now, hurry up, we don't have much time.''

He checked the wall clock. ''Mom, we have two hours.''

''When you have to rely on public transportation, you have to leave early. Too bad your Duster's in the shop. When did that nebbish mechanic say it would be ready?''

Sam shrugged. ''Sometime soon,'' he mumbled through a mouthful of potatoes.

''Look, now watch. I want you to tell me what you think about these steps leading up to Marty's entrance.'' She set herself between the table and the kitchen counter, brow furrowed in concentration. ''This was the original way I choreographed it.'' Her heels scraped against the linoleum as she slid twice to the right, twirled, then opened her arms to accept her partner. ''These are the changes I made tonight.'' Instead of sliding, she spun twice on one toe, graceful as a ballerina, then drew her arms up in an arc, palms open in welcome. ''It's much more dramatic, don't you think?''

''It looks fine, Mom.'' Sam wiped his mouth with his napkin, then got up to throw the chicken bones into the trash.

"But do you think it's better?"

"I . . . never saw you dance with such . . . finesse." He put his silverware and dishes into the sink, then soaped up a sponge. "Didn't you eat?"

"Earlier I had a little something. I'm too nervous." She continued to work on the new steps as Sam finished the dishes. "I hope Marty likes this. He's the one who said the entrance needed some pizazz. How was work?"

Sam turned, drying his hand on a dishtowel. "It was great. Did you get the application form from the bank?"

Gerda froze in mid-step. Placing one hand against her lips, her eyes went wide. "I forgot," she said in a small voice. "I was there too, cashing my check. Oh, dammit!"

"That's okay. Maybe you could just ask him his last name tonight."

"I don't think so, honey. When we're dancing, Marty is . . . Marty. He never offers much personal information and I never pry." A touch of sadness tinged her smile. "We're just out to have fun."

"It's okay, Mom." He stole a look at the clock again, cleared his throat and said in a booming Dudley Do-Right voice, "Hey, look at the time. What are you doing just standing there?"

"Huh?"

He took her arm and hustled her out of the kitchen. "You've got a rehearsal to go to. Don't want to be late, do you?"

They stopped by the door, her laughter bubbling up like water in a pot, threatening to overflow.

"What's so funny?" he said in the same cartoon voice, but then lost it. He giggled at first, then joined her in mirthful howls that caused him to double over. Tears ran down his cheeks.

"Oh, god, I'm gonna ruin my makeup." She sniffed and

let loose with another spate of chuckles. ‘‘You’re so damn funny, Noah.’’

‘‘Yeah, well, sometimes I have to be.’’

She gave him a questioning look and opened her mouth to speak. ‘‘Better get your jacket,’’ he said. She ran into the other room, returning with both their jackets and her purse. Sam locked the door behind them, and whistled ‘‘Lullaby of Broadway’’ as he followed Gerda down the stairs.

CHAPTER SIXTEEN

With her red sequined dress and matching shoes and purse, Gerda had looked like a duchess in a ghetto, riding the subway train. She caught her share of curious stares on the way to the city, but ignored them, chatting away with Sam in a corner seat and studying her newly manicured nails. But here at the Starlight, they were in a different world. Here, Gerda was not a curiosity, she fit right in. If anything, it was Sam who was the odd one out, underdressed in Noah's mint green shirt and charcoal gray trousers.

Forties swing music pounded from the bandstand, its infectious rhythms forcing the middle-aged patrons to grab their partners and vie for a place on the dance floor. These dancers didn't need an Accelerator chamber to transport them back to that long-gone era; the songs they cherished from their youth brought them to it with greater ease and a lot less expense.

Gerda's eyes swept the room. She squinted toward the dance floor, then, turning, did a slow double take and clicked her tongue. Sam followed her gaze and saw Mary Jane Wax, wearing a plain gray dress, leaning against the wall. Hugging her purse against her chest, she blinked with myopic longing at the dancers.

"I *told* her," Gerda groaned. "Do you think she'd listen to me?"

Sam hitched one shoulder and opened his mouth to speak, but Gerda was already halfway to the cause of her consternation. There was nothing he could do but follow her through the crowd.

"Mary Jane Wax!" Gerda stood with her hands on her hips, jutting out her chin. "Get your butt closer to that dance floor."

Mary Jane cringed, the large eyes behind her brown-framed glasses seeking Sam's help. "Hi, Noah," she said quietly.

"Hi, Mary Jane. It's nice to—"

"How do you expect to get a fellow to dance with you if you stand here like a glop of mud?" Gerda groused.

"I . . ."

Mary Jane was not the only lost soul in the room. Other women milled around the entrance, their eyes hopeful as each unattached male passed by. Loneliness. It was a powerful adversary. Gerda knew how it felt to be in its grip and could identify with Mary Jane's plight very well. She put her arm through Mary Jane's and started to lead her toward the floor, but Mary held back, biting her lip, a glimmer of tears shining behind her thick lenses.

Sam stepped in front of them. "Would you like to dance, Mary Jane?"

She looked up at him, surprised. "I don't know. I mean, it's been so long since I've been out on a dance floor."

Sam smiled. "Same here, but I'm willing to give it a try if you are."

"Noah, don't be silly." Gerda grumbled. "You don't dance."

"Who told you that?" He gently removed Gerda's arm from Mary Jane's and drew the befuddled Mary Jane into his arms. For a moment she didn't respond, but then her arms gradually rose to circle Sam's back. Her left hand still clutched her purse. Her nose brushed the middle button of his shirt as they swayed to "Moonlight Serenade."

Sighing, Sam let his eyes wander. Three mirror balls rotated over the dance floor, glinting and gleaming; the effect was mesmerizing. Staring at them, Sam had the feeling that time had frozen. In this world, Gerda was happy, optimistic and would always be young, Here, there could be no disappointment, no heartbreaking end to the song.

"Excuse me." A tall man with curly salt-and-pepper hair tapped Sam on the shoulder. "May I cut in?"

"Jason." Mary Jane beamed at the man. She mouthed a thank-you to Sam as she stepped into Jason's arms. Sam bowed and shuffled backward to give them room, almost backing into another couple. Cheeks burning, he mumbled his apologies, then made his way off the dance floor.

"That worked out well," he said, returning to Gerda's side.

"Jason finally got up the nerve, huh? God knows, they both probably would have sprung roots if they held up those walls any longer."

Sam chuckled.

Gerda's eyes were on the door, the mirror ball reflections traveling across her face. Her sequined dress winked and glimmered. *Marty?* She mouthed the question, her eyes searching, pushing through the crowd.

Two couples approached her as she stood at the edge of the dance floor. They were regulars here, she whispered to Sam: Andy, Louise, Georgie and Marge. They were excited for her, and asked after Marty, telling her they would be here three nights from now to cheer them both on. Arm in arm, the couples moved on toward the dance floor, while Gerda's hopeful gaze fell on the door again.

"He should have been here by now." She bounced on her toes, alternately wringing her hands and grasping Sam's sleeve.

"Would you like to dance?" Sam asked, placing a calming hand on her shoulder.

"Noah, what is with you lately?"

"Don't think I didn't learn something watching you knocking 'em dead at the Wildwood all those years." The orchestra was blasting "Papa Loves Mambo." Apparently, so did Gerda. She found the rhythm of the dance with ease, Sam following along the best he could. "Smile, you guys!" A camera's flash caused him to lose the beat momentarily. But he was soon back in form. Either they didn't look too shabby or Gerda was well known for her dancing prowess. She was in the spotlight now. The other dancers in their vicinity formed a circle around them, shouting their encouragements as Gerda lost herself in the music. Dancing was like breathing to her: she didn't have to think about the steps, her feet knew where to move her, her body was well versed on all the proper gyrations. Sweat dappled her forehead as the horns blared. Sam wasn't a bad dancer (although he couldn't remember where he had picked up that particular talent), but even Fred Astaire would have had a job keeping up with Gerda Ellman. Giving up, he drifted back into the sidelines as the music shifted to a cha-cha. Gerda followed its lead, not missing a beat.

Screeeeeech!

Sam's head whipped toward the noise, which brayed from the far corner of the room. It sounded like a bullhorn crackle. A bullhorn? In a dance hall? Another squawk rattled the rafters, with a dollop of feedback thrown in this time. Sam stood on his toes, straining to see over the crowd. The fingernails-on-the-blackboard sound had drowned out the music. He'd heard it. Why hadn't anyone else? Unless . . .

Screech! *What we want is to be treated fairly.* Squawk. *The management has proposed a five-percent wage increase, which we deem to be unacceptable . . .*

Had the Starlight's workers taken this moment to call a strike?

"What's the matter, honey?" Gerda's solo was over. She dug a tissue from her clutch purse and dabbed at her forehead and neck. The music had changed to a waltz.

Dammit, Ziggy. You're really pushing it!

"Mom, would you like some water?" Through a gap in the dancers, Sam spied Al standing by the water fountain, lambasting the handlink with a fury Sam had rarely seem him exhibit.

You're gonna pay for this, you reeking pile of scrap metal!

"Sure, Noah. Marty usually brings me a cup after we dance, but . . . he's not here yet." Her eyes begged for comfort, for him to tell her everything would be all right. He wished he could say those words and really mean them. Instead he bent to give her a quick hug.

"I'll be right back," he assured her, but her gaze was already back on the door.

Sam weaved through the throng, reaching the water fountain just in time to hear a list of strikers' demands bellow from the link. Al glared at the thing, wide-eyed, dazed, his hair sticking up in short dark tufts. "I'm gonna kill her, Sam. This time she's really done it."

"She's . . . on strike?"

"Yeah. She wants Gooshie back, and to help her in her cause she's enlisted the help of every organized labor union since the beginning of time. Her hero of the hour is Jimmy Hoffa."

. . . *an end to wage freezing*—screeee!

"And in another minute she's gonna be wearing his cement boots."

Sam edged deeper into the corner as a woman clad in a purple spangled dress bent to take a drink. "Well, why don't you let Gooshie in on the problem?"

"I wanted to give him some time, Sam. He's got something on his mind he really doesn't want to talk about. If I go after him now, he might just skip town for good."

Scrrreeeeeiiiiiissssssh!

"Shaddup." Al whacked the link on its side. "I was gonna stick around and take a look at this Marty guy, but it doesn't look like he's gonna show."

"I know, Al. He's already forty-five minutes late."

"Hey, how did your first day on the job go?"

"It went really well."

Al nodded and threw him a lascivious wink. "Uh-huh. I'll bet it did."

Look for the union label!

"That's *it*!" Al jabbed the code into the keypad, then rammed the link into his jacket pocket. Sam could still hear the muffled refrains of the rally song as Al backed into the white light of the imaging chamber. "I'm not gonna be able to help you until I get this sorted out. Just do the best you can until I get back."

Sam exhaled slowly, watching his friend leave. He shook his head, unable to resist giving in to the smile that was tugging at the corners of his mouth. Ziggy deciding to strike was an inconvenience, but it was also pretty hilarious. Another rule of thumb: to survive as a Leaper, one must have a highly developed sense of humor. He slipped a cup out of the dispenser on the wall and filled it with water. Easing his way back through the crowd, he prayed Gerda would no longer be waiting by the door, and that he would find her and Marty on the dance floor hotfooting it to the beat of "Chattanooga Choo Choo."

She was not by the entrance, which caused Sam's optimism to grow. Maybe Marty had arrived. Maybe they were dancing. He scanned the dance floor, but she was nowhere in sight. After a futile search of every corner of the room, he gave up and ambled into the lobby. There he found her seated on a bench by the coat room, scrutinizing her nails. Her jacket and Noah's were folded neatly on her lap. "Hi, baby. You ready?" she asked. Her eyes were very bright, her face almost as red as her hair.

Sam shrugged. "For what?"

"To go home."

Sam handed her the cup of water. "Here."

She waved it away. "Feh."

"Come on. It'll cool you off."

She took it from him resignedly and drank it down in one gulp.

"Better?" he asked.

"No." She crumpled it in her fist, then dropped it on the bench.

"Wanna come back in there and dance with me?"

"No."

"Sure you do." He brought their coats back to the coat check. "You know, this night doesn't have to be a total loss. What if we rehearse the dance? I'll bet I can learn it in no time and then—'' He turned toward her, but she was no longer on the bench. The crumpled paper cup remained, but she was by the door, throwing her arms around a man at least thirty years her junior, who barely came up to the top of her head. He held her at arm's length, then placed a hand on his chest, making a great show of catching his breath. They looked good together, comfortable, like a long-married couple greeting each other at the end of the day. She helped him remove his jacket, flung it over her arm, then clicked open her purse. The man raised his eyebrows and chuckled, as though this was a routine he tolerated each time they met. He clasped his hands behind his back, opening his mouth wide as she unwrapped a stick of gum and placed it on his tongue.

Her smile could have lit up the entire city, as she led her friend over to Sam. ''Marty, I'd like you to meet my son, Noah.'' Her eyes still glimmered, now with excitement instead of tears.

Sam shook Marty's hand, which was cool and somewhat moist. *Now! Ask him now!* the voice in Sam's head demanded. But Sam's tongue was frozen. His jaw dropped, as if a lead weight were housed in his chin.

''It's . . . nice to meet you, Noah.'' Marty threw Gerda an uncertain look. He was no Casanova. His hair, an indiscriminate brown, was slicked back with enough grease to keep an axle rotating smoothly for days. The hint of a paunch crept over his wide belt. He wore a tan leisure suit and black shoes. His eyes were blue, nearly bugging out of his head. Googly eyes. *Must have caught hell in school for looking like that,* Sam thought.

''Are you okay?'' Marty asked.

Again, Sam tried to speak, but Marty's abominable bad breath, battling its way through the scent of his peppermint gum, stopped him. Suddenly he didn't want to be around this Marty at all. He took a step back, then two more, the exit door cool against his back. It wasn't just the man's halitosis driving him away—no, it was something else, something that would come to him if he just had a chance to think . . .

"Noah, stop acting so ridiculous and watch us do 'Lullaby.' " Gerda's voice echoed from somewhere far away.

Marty was watching him, concern making his eyes go even buggier. "Uh . . . you okay?"

That voice . . .

"I . . ." Sam's eyes flicked toward Gerda, then back to Marty. ". . . think so."

"Come on." Gerda seized Marty's arm and pulled him toward the ballroom. "We're wasting time."

"Wait a minute now. Just let me check my coat." He took it off her arm, brought it to the check room, then returned and took her hand.

Sam followed them inside, and couldn't help noticing how their presence altered the mood of the room. Conversations stopped and dancers slowed their steps, clearing a path for them. Gerda flowed over to the bandleader and whispered something in his ear. He signaled to the orchestra to stop the music, then smiled and stepped up to the microphone. "You're in for a treat, folks. The couple you'll be cheering on three nights from now is going to give us a sneak preview of their 'You Can Be a Star' audition number, 'Lullaby of Broadway.' " In the corner next to the bandstand, Gerda was showing Marty the new steps she had created for his entrance. He followed her lead, acing it on the first try.

"So will you please clear the floor and give a warm Starlight Ballroom welcome to Gerda and Marty!"

The crowd whistled and cheered, then situated themselves on the sidelines to watch.

As the orchestra played the jaunty introduction, Gerda was transformed. Like a snake shedding its skin, she threw off all remnants of Gerda Ellman, anonymous Brooklynite homemaker, to become Gerda Ellman . . . the star. Sam stood watching from the sidelines, falling under her spell, as she belted out the tune with the confidence and zeal of a seasoned Broadway diva. Marty was watching too as he did a slow soft-shoe behind her. Those strange eyes were filled with a longing Sam had never seen in them before.

Before? But I don't know him . . .

Marty took his cue, using the new step Gerda had shown him. They spun together toward the middle of the floor. Their dancing was like flowing water—inhaling, exhaling, rolling down a hill. Effortless and free. They were not a pair of dancers rehearsing for a show, but lovers in their own world, each step and twirl a proclamation of feeling. They were so very right together.

When it was over, Sam still had not found his voice. Gerda and Marty were shaking hands with well-wishers as they approached him. Her eyes were still shining, now filled with the anticipation of what was to come three nights from now, and with the unbridled excitement of being with the man she so obviously loved.

Sam forced himself to step forward and shake hands with both of them. "That was . . . amazing."

"What did I tell you, isn't he the best?" she gushed.

"Yeah," Sam looked down, rubbing his forehead. "Listen, I've got to leave."

He felt Marty's strange eyes on him.

"Noah, what is the matter?" Gerda placed her palm against his brow.

"Are you feeling ill?" Marty asked.

"No. It's just . . . just . . ." *You.* "Could you see that she gets home okay?"

"Sure—"

"Thanks," Sam said, heading for the door. "Thanks a lot."

Sam raced into the lobby, then pushed open the outer door. A blast of autumn's chill made his teeth chatter, reminding him he had forgotten his jacket. But the thought of turning back made him shiver even harder. He flew down the steps and didn't slow until he collapsed on a bench on the subway platform.

CHAPTER SEVENTEEN

It was too early for supper, too late for lunch. A lone admiral sat in the corner table of the commissary, sipping at his second cup of coffee. His thoughts were not on his paramour, his time-traveling friend or Brooklyn, New York, in 1978, but on a television show called *The Prisoner*. The show was one of those cult classics from the sixties so many of the techs were gaga over. They would take over the fifty-seat theater on the third floor and run a couple of tapes a night until they had viewed the entire series. Then they'd have these ridiculous, pseudo-intellectual conversations about it, like it was a real slice of history. One night, needing to immerse himself in some mindless diversion, Al had strolled into one of the viewing parties. What he saw then came to mind now: in the Village, a deceptively happy place where the Prisoner was kept, televison transmissions and music broadcasts blared any time of the day or night at the whim of a mysterious entity known as Number Two. Al set his coffee down and leaned his head on the table, realizing that right now, he was The Prisoner, and Ziggy was doing a magnificent impression of that irritating, all-knowing jailer. Her song selection of the moment was some little ditty called "Part of the Union." Where was she digging up this stuff? The monitor above the food service counter showed a hollow-eyed Jimmy Hoffa spurring on the crowd at a Teamsters rally.

Al groaned, wishing he were in Vegas. Hell, right now, he'd settle for sitting at a taco stand in Albuquerque, sipping a ginger ale.

"This seat taken?"

He raised his head. Verbeena Beeks, the project psychologist, stood across the table, tray in hand.

"Well?"

"Hey, Beena. Siddown."

She set her tray opposite his half-empty coffee cup. He squinted at her selection of salad and yogurt, then at her. "I'll bet when no one's looking you order those belly-bomb burgers Felix loves to tantalize us with."

"Not me." She squeezed a dollop of low-fat Italian dressing from a small packet onto her salad. "How are you holding up?"

He shrugged, not even attempting to fake a smile. She would have seen right through it anyway. "I don't know what to do. I've tried threats, insults. I've even tried ignoring her. Nothing works."

"You know, Al, attempting to analyze Ziggy is no more difficult than trying to analyze you."

''How so?'' He twiddled the stirrer in what remained of his coffee.

''Well, Ziggy is an extention of you, after all. Sam used a sampling of your brain cells as well as his own to fashion a portion of her human characteristics.''

''So?''

Verbeena speared a lettuce leaf with her fork, then pointed it at him. ''Your mother abandoned you as a child. Ziggy was abandoned once too—by her father. Sam.''

Al squirmed, suddenly feeling the itch to be tossing out dice at a craps table. ''I don't like where you're going, Beena.''

''Now she's been left again by Gooshie, the human she regards as basically . . . her soul mate.''

''You're romanticizing the hell out of this.'' Al crossed his arms and looked away.

''I don't know about that.''

''You are!''

''I thinketh thou dost protesteth too much.'' She popped the lettuce in her mouth, and crunched on it grandly.

She was right, dammit. Verbeena was right about stuff like this ninety-eight percent of the time. It was that infuriating talent of winding her way inside her patients' heads that had convinced Sam to hire her way back when. Al recalled scanning her résumé after Sam had interviewed her. It was filled with accolades from her professors and glowing references from her previous employer, and Al immediately agreed with Sam's decision to bring her on board. His discomfort around her came only after getting a look at her sable skin and those eyes that could penetrate his soul. He realized then there was nothing she couldn't eke out of him if she had a mind to, and when something was troubling him, she was the last person he'd seek out. Since his return from Nam, all shrinks made him uneasy.

They poked and prodded your gray matter, not giving up until they pulled some deep, dark (painful) secret out of you, a secret you had repressed and never wanted to remember anyway. He was quite happy to work out his problems on his own now. But this time he hadn't been cagey enough to lay low, and Verbeena had found him.

"Ziggy thinks Gooshie's not coming back. And she's as afraid of abandonment as you are," she said calmly, cutting her cherry tomato into neat quarters.

Al rubbed his face, then glared at her. "True or not true, it doesn't solve our problem."

"It's a step in the right direction."

"I'm open to suggestions. What do wc do next?" he asked, but he had a feeling he knew.

"Ziggy has to be assured that Gooshie would never leave her for good. And she has to be told this by him."

Al got up and tossed his cup in the trash. "He spoke to her before he left."

"Obviously whatever he said didn't make much of an impression. You should go to him, Al. Let him in on what's going on here. He has too much invested in Ziggy, emotionally and professionally, not to care."

He gave her a hard look. "How do you know I know where he is?"

She gave her lips three delicate dabs with her napkin. "You had to track him, Al. You couldn't rest easy not knowing where he is. As many times as you take out your frustrations on Gooshie, you care about him. A lot."

Bang! Zoom! She had him again.

"Yogurt?" She offered him the unopened container.

"Nah."

"For the road?"

He checked his watch. If he left now, he could be in Verdad by seven o'clock. The town was only seventy-five miles away, so tiny it had probably been added as an afterthought to his pocket map of New Mexico. Yeah, he would go. At least now he'd find out why Gooshie had decided to hole up in such a cesspool.

"It's blueberry swirl." Verbena jiggled the container.

"Fruit on the bottom?"

"Of course."

He took it from her, then tossed it in the air and caught it as he headed for the commissary's double doors. The thought of wringing Gooshie's neck made his steps a little lighter.

"Al?" she called.

He turned. "Yeah?"

She wagged a finger. "Be nice."

He grimaced, touching his left temple. She *could* read his mind. Sometimes he thought he felt those mental fingers poking his gray matter even when he wasn't with her. Now he was sure of it. Still, he refused to give her the benefit of letting her know *he* knew the power she wielded. "I'm always nice," he said.

"Uh-huh." Smiling, she threw him a wink, and dug into her salad again.

CHAPTER EIGHTEEN

Her safe spot was so far away. The sand went on for miles, and the sun was so bright she had to shade her eyes to see the shoreline. The fruits were laid out on their picnic blanket, as she had come to expect. But other items dotted the landscape, items so incongruous with their surroundings that Rebecca took their presence as a warning. Over there was a metal shopping cart, its arched handle gleaming. Farther out was a stuffed frog, with bulging black eyes and spotted skin. By her feet lay a string of plastic monkeys, attached to one another by their hooked tails.

"It's all so interesting today, isn't it?" the voice sang in her right ear.

The sand stretched out another foot, making her entrails

go cold. She was even farther away from her safe spot now.

"You'll need to take more than those one step, two steps this time. That's for babies, don't you think? You've come so far, you should be proud of yourself . . ."

A great pressure against her back forced her to stumble forward. Her limbs would not respond to her commands; instead they jerked her across the endless sand as if she were a marionette. The fruits rolled out of their basket, following at her heels, like alien pets. She waited to hear the sickening wet pop as they exploded, and feel the searing pain as those cherry pits assaulted her. Nothing, nothing.

The cart hurtled toward her like a banshee on a motorbike, its rattle as earsplitting as a war cry. She would have liked to run from it, but her legs had other ideas—forcing her forward in a herky-jerky dance. The cart slowed, just shy of careening into her side, then took its place beside the pineapples, cherries and plums, rolling, rolling along.

Any other time, the whole scene might have seemed hilarious, but now . . .

. . . something long and cold was crawling up her back. She screamed as it touched the nape of her neck, as it draped itself around her throat like a lei. Her spastic fingers flailed at it, discovering it was the string of monkeys, swaying and clicking against one another, like brittle bones.

Her safe spot was nowhere in sight. She'd thought she'd see it by now, but . . .

The stuffed frog joined the parade. It didn't croak, so much as growl, opening its mouth wide to reveal needle-sharp teeth.

Far away she heard the water lapping on the shoreline—her safe spot. Far away. Everything was slowing down. Her consorts surrounded her, quivering with wicked anticipation. The frog's eyes wiggled like jellied eggs. Something terrible was going to happen, because these . . . things were drawing closer; the monkeys wrapped themselves tighter and tighter around her throat. She could no longer hear the lazy lapping of the water. Her safe spot was gone. Gone!

"Ma-maaaa!"

Rebecca gasped. Her heart thrummed so wildly she was afraid it would seize up on her and simply stop. She clenched her sweat-soaked hair and heaved deep, throat-closing sobs. Tears rained down her cheeks, dripping off her like beads of sweat, saturating her comforter. She forced herself to lie down and slough her way through her post-dream ritual. Slowly a sense of semi-calm stole over her.

The nightmare had never terrified her as much as this. She could always find her safe spot, no matter how horrific the imagery, no matter how persistently the voice taunted her. She opened her eyes, her gaze touching the early morning shadows on the ceiling. Her life was going well now, better than it had for so many months. Why should she feel so threatened? Noah suddenly came to mind. Rebecca breathed deeply, thinking of his intense look—lips pressed together, brow knitting in concentration—as he plowed through those monstrous piles of paperwork. Yesterday, she had stolen glances at him many times, hoping they might have lunch together, but he left the house before she could suggest it. *See? These are dangerous thoughts. It was thinking about Noah that caused your subconscious to grow sharper fangs and heighten its attack . . .*

But thinking about him made her happy. He had a funny, contagious quirk of a smile. That one lock of hair always falling over his brow begged her all day yesterday to smooth it back.

These are dangerous thoughts!

On her bureau the luminous hands on the clock told her it was only six-thirty. She let out a long cleansing breath, wiping her face with her blanket. Falling back onto her pillow, she was grateful to have another hour to recover. Her toes ached. In her terror she must have had them clenched the whole time. The scabs beneath the bandages on her palms pained her; she must have tried to dig her nails into herself again.

She was so glad for the workday, and that Noah would arrive in another two and a half hours. She watched the glow of the rose pink sunrise limn the edges of the closed venetian blinds. As the minutes ticked on, the flush grew warmer, deeper. She recalled the warmth of the sun's rays against her cheeks and brow. She was able to melt into that memory with ease. And that too made her glad.

CHAPTER NINETEEN

Sam sat in Gerda's living room with *Good Morning America* turned low on the TV. The Middle East summit was all over the news. A beaming Jimmy Carter stood between Anwar Sadat and Manachem Begin, the peace talks a real feather in the previously unpopular president's cap. But the news was ancient history to Sam, offering him no insights, no surprises. His interest flagged and he tuned it out, thinking again of the little man with the funny eyes Gerda cared for so much. Sam still couldn't figure out why the sight of the guy made him turn on his heels and run. So many times he relied on his gut feelings to push him in the right direction. In this case, the right direction was anywhere that

Marty wasn't. And the sixty-five-thousand dollar question was "Why?"

His eyes felt as if they'd been rubbed raw with sandpaper. Yawning, he pinched the bridge of his nose, hoping the pounding in his temples would fade as the morning progressed. After tossing and turning most of the night, he had finally fallen into an exhausted doze at six A.M., and slept until the alarm buzz woke him at eight forty-five. He shouldn't have done that. That small respite had made him even more tired, and he knew he would suffer for it all day. But that was the least of his problems.

Gerda wasn't home. He thought he'd heard her come in last night, but he'd feigned sleep, wanting to hold off their inevitable confrontation until the morning. *I really blew it this time,* he thought, sipping at his coffee. *She probably wonders why her son acted like such a loon. She'll definitely want a good explanation as to why I ran out of the ballroom last night. I can't very well tell her the truth—that I have this niggling sensation in my gut that my hanging around Marty would be detrimental to this Leap. I wish I knew why. I wish Al would pop in right now so I could just talk to him. Even if he had no answers, at least he'd listen.* Sam sighed, squeezing his eyes shut, trying to summon Al mentally (which had never worked before, as far as he knew, but there was always a first time). He was rewarded by a most welcome image of Rebecca Wexler's blue eyes. He opened his eyes slowly, a weary smile pulling at the corners of his lips. Mayor Ed Koch was on the TV now, asking "How'm I doin'?"

"Hopefully, a lot better than I am," Sam mumbled.

He couldn't sit anymore. Sitting made him think, and thinking made him edgy. After clicking off the TV, he went into the kitchen to rinse out his cup. Maybe he should leave Gerda a note, apologizing. He folded his arms over the counter, wondering how he was going to fix things for this woman when he couldn't manage a simple, friendly conversation with Marty.

He wished he had an answer; he wished Al were here.

Checking the clock, he found it was still early. But he would start out for Rebecca's house anyway. The cool morning air might clear his head. And tonight he'd face Gerda and hopefully be able to pick up where he left off . . .

He grabbed his jacket off the kitchen chair and made his way to the front door. Pulling it open, he found Gerda on the other side, digging in her large shoulder bag.

She looked up, surprised. "Noah?"

He took a step back. "Hi, Mom."

She entered the apartment, then padded into the kitchen. "I was hoping I'd see you before you left for work. Can I talk to you?" she called.

"Uh . . . sure."

He loped into the kitchen, shoving his hands into his pockets. She stood by the table, continuing to search the depths of her bag. "I want to apologize to you for last night."

Sam's eyes widened. He pressed his hand to his chest. "Apologize . . . to me?"

"You really are Little Sir Echo."

"Sorry . . . it's just that . . ."

"I understand how uncomfortable you must have felt, seeing me act that way, all giggly and excited like a schoolgirl. But I have to tell you, last night was wonderful. Marty and me, we had the best time. I don't think I've ever laughed so much."

"That's . . . great."

"But you still didn't get to talk with Marty, and I didn't do much to help get the conversation started." She shook her head. "It was wrong of me. I should have acted more adult. I'm really sorry. I wanted to make it up to you, so I went out early and got this.'' She pulled a brown envelope from her bag and handed it to him.

''What's this?''

''Open it.''

He smoothed the envelope between his fingers. In the upper right-hand corner, ''You Can Be a Star'' was printed in brick red letters. Beneath that was a post office box address in Los Angeles, California. ''It's the application.''

''Yes.'' She smiled slightly. ''I owed you that much, at least.''

His eyes moved to the envelope, then back to her, before settling on the envelope again.

''Go ahead.''

He started at the corner. With great care, he ripped the edge, then slid his thumb beneath the paper, opening the flap . . .

CHAPTER TWENTY

Miles Davis. Now there was a musician. Too bad he was dead. All the best ones were now, weren't they? Damn shame. Al tapped his fingers against the steering wheel of his Ferrari. As he raced along the desert highway, the air-conditioning kept him as cool as the music. And the music was swingin', alive. Real. Al had picked up the newly re-mastered issue of Miles's *Kind of Blue* the last time he was cajoled into accompanying Tina on a shopping trip to Albuquerque. She'd come back so loaded down with packages, Al had to fit five overflowing shopping bags in the backseat when he ran out of room in the trunk. His purchases that day were slightly less extreme: a teal-colored fedora and the CD he was now diggin'.

He glanced at the screen of the surveillance kit nestled on the passenger seat. The kit was housed inside a square suitcase so well fortified with steel innards it would take nothing less than a few rounds from an Uzi to destroy it. The kit had been sitting behind his desk after he returned from the imaging chamber a few months back. Where it came from, Al never found out. Sometimes things changed during Sam's Leaps. Items appeared, items disappeared. Relationships were altered. Thankfully, no one but him and Ziggy realized the changes had taken place, or major chaos might have ensued. Al had long ago stopped worrying about what was in store for him each time he exited the chamber. It was like turning on TV during sweeps time—there was always a new twist, a (sometimes) welcome surprise or two.

The blip that was Gooshie had not deviated from its position since it froze in place yesterday evening. Al knew the programmer wouldn't stray too far, but he could not have predicted he would have gone to Verdad. The town was seventy-five miles south of the Project, and not a vacation hot spot by any means. Al had passed through there once on the way to Vegas. It was a dusty rat trap of a place, with a single-pump gas station, a bar, a bar, and another bar thrown in for good measure. What Gooshie was doing in a place like that, Al couldn't begin to imagine. But he'd find out soon enough, get Gooshie to make nice to Ziggy over the modem of the laptop, and end this ridiculous strike once and for all. It was impossible not to be optimistic enjoying the silky smoothness of the ride and the music. Cool man cool, Al breathed, flipping up the visor and enjoying how the sand, the scrub brush and the shadows zipped by him in a silent blur.

• • •

Verdad was not as awful as Al remembered. It was worse. He drove slowly through the nearly deserted streets, checking Gooshie's location in relationship to his. Surprisingly, the programmer was very close, probably around the next turn. What was he doing in this stinkhole? Unless this was all a ploy, unless cagey ol' Gooshie had known of Al's devious plot, removed his clothing and toiletries, dumped the bugged suitcase in a wastebasket, then taken off to Vegas.

Kind of Blue had ended a little while ago, but Al hadn't popped in another CD or flipped on the radio. He was too keen on getting to the bottom of this. Besides, not a whole hell of a lot could follow Miles.

A grizzle-chinned, barechested geezer with leathery skin staggered into the center of the road, causing Al to slow the Ferrari to a crawl. Weaving back and forth, Geezer flashed a smile revealing four rotten teeth, then took wobbly aim at the Ferrari with his beer bottle.

"*Hey!*" Al's heart clenched as he squealed to a stop. But before he could free himself from his seat restraint, Geezer pitched the bottle at the windshield with a strength and delivery that would have done Nolan Ryan proud.

"*Goddammit!*" Al pounded his fist on the dash as the passenger side of the windshield took the brunt of the assault. The bottle bounced off the glass, leaving a spiderweb crack. Rolling off the hood, it landed in the road, swirling up a small eddy of dirt.

"*You son of a bitch!*" Gritting his teeth, Al pushed the door open and exploded out of the car, thinking he should save the bottle as a souvenir of how ridiculous this day had become. The old guy was doubled over, clasping his knees and cackling like the Wicked Witch of the West. Al stopped in his tracks. Did he really want to confront this sotted old wretch? The smell of the guy's breath alone would probably be enough to knock him over. He had no time for this. If he had to confront someone with stinkbreath, it would be Gooshie and no one else.

He returned to the car and checked his surveillance map before revving up the engine. ''Next time, you lousy old coot,'' he shouted out the window, reveling in the disappointment on the old guy's face. Throwing out a few choice epithets for good measure, Al burned rubber as he peeled around the corner.

He was almost there. The Ferrari dot was closing in on the Gooshie dot at a good clip. The only problem was, nothing was coming up dead ahead that told him where Gooshie might be. A few half-demolished storefronts, their windows boarded up with splintered wood and ''Condemned'' signs lined either side of the road. He tapped the accelerator with the toe of his red shoe, trying his best to ignore the ruined side of the windshield. A sharp turn loomed. He twisted the wheel and found the mother lode—a babydoll pink house with pale blue shutters standing alone on the corner of the dusty street. The shutters' paint was chipped, the siding was splintered and peeling in spots, but the porch looked freshly painted. Despite its deterioration, the house had a lived-in quality. And the street certainly had that civilized look—whiskey bottles, beer cans and an interesting collection of other debris dotted the heat-ravaged landscape. *This must be the place*, Al thought. The Gooshie blip had become one with the Ferrari's, and the map didn't lie.

A driveway, which was more like a smaller version of a parking lot, beckoned from the left side of the house. It was three-quarters filled with pickup trucks, Chevys, a babydoll pink Cadillac and Gooshie's Honda looking very out of place parked next to the Caddy. What kind of people living out in the middle of nowhere had this many guests?

Al steered into a spot close to the street. He didn't plan on staying any longer than it took Gooshie to convince his "soul mate" to cut the crap.

With a grunt, he pushed open the car door and glared at the cracked windshield, then at the pair of dots continuing to blink like dual heartbeats. *All right, Gooshie. Here I come. You better not give me any trouble or I'll head back into town and sic ol' Leatherpuss on you.* He was about to get out when he remembered the laptop. After retrieving it from under the front seat and locking the car door after him, he pulled a cigar from his shirt pocket. He stuck it between his teeth, then tramped a disgruntled path to the house, kicking at beer cans along the way.

CHAPTER TWENTY-ONE

"Noah? NO-ah! Talk to me. You look like you've seen a ghost." Gerda was tugging at his sleeve, but Sam hardly felt it. He was still focused on the name on the application form.

"If you don't tell me what the matter is right now, I'm gonna call a doctor."

Irving Gushman, 280 West Eighth Street, Third Floor, New York, New York. Telephone (212) 555-7073.

"It's . . . nothing, Mom. I have . . . *had* a friend who lived at the same address as Goosh—uh—Irving."

"Oh." Gerda gave him a bewildered smile. "Do you think they might know each other?"

"Oh, no, Mom, no. It was a long time ago. Gee, look at the time. I'd better get going."

Ignoring her befuddlement, he kissed her cheek, then raced down the stairs. He needed to get to a phone booth and thought he recalled passing one yesterday on the way to Rebecca's. He turned the half-rusted handle of the ancient wooden door leading outside, but the door wouldn't budge. Groaning with frustration, he twisted the handle again, pushing his shoulder against the door once, twice, until it gave with a creak and a bang.

Stumbling down the steps to the sidewalk, he caught his breath, then ran in the direction of his workplace. *Gooshie!* He was one person from the Project Sam remembered, with varying degrees of lucidity. Sam doubted that the name on the paper by itself would have struck a chord. But the combination of seeing that name and equating it with the face from the night before brought the memory of Gooshie crashing home.

Sometimes Sam confused Gooshie with other control room technicians who popped up in his conversations with Al. But last night, subconsciously, Sam knew exactly who Gerda's partner was. *Gooshie!* The name was as familiar to Sam as Al's. It came hurtling from the hologram's mouth when he needed data pronto or was exasperated to the point of coming to human-to-handlink blows with Ziggy.

Now Gooshie was here, years before the Project had even been a sparkle in Sam's potent gray matter. In 1978, Sam was twenty-five years old, finishing up his doctorate work. And Gooshie was . . . dancing at the Starlight, a student at NYU . . . what else, Sam didn't know.

He ran two long blocks, but wasn't even winded. All he wanted was to get to that phone booth. He spied it halfway down the next block. He scurried across the intersection, almost getting sideswiped by a yellow cab in the process. The driver was screaming words much too crude for the early hour. But the epithets didn't faze Sam; he was a man possessed as he closed the distance. Three . . . two . . . one. He reached the booth, and clung to its side, as if it were a life preserver on a sinking ship. His throat burned as he struggled to catch his breath, his heart trip-hammered. *Yes.*

The door squealed in protest as he pushed it open. He didn't bother sitting on the little metal seat as he fished the application from his pocket. *555-7073.* Mumbling the number over and over, he shoved the paper into his trouser pocket, then licked his lips and lifted the receiver. The dial tone burred in his ear as he pushed a dime halfway into the slot. He stared at the coin, then at the receiver, as if it were an alien being growing out of his palm. He couldn't do this. Not now, anyway. He had run out of the ballroom for the same reason he was hesitating now. The dial tone faded as he slowly, reluctantly, placed the receiver back into its cradle. What if he met with Gooshie and said the wrong thing? His actions could jeopardize the success of the Project. Gooshie's part in its inception was crucial. Sam may have created Ziggy, but Gooshie maintained her as no one else could have. His conversations with her kept her at an intellectual peak. Gooshie was her friend, her confidant and sounding board.

No. Sam sighed. The risk was too great. Strange things happened when you tampered with the space-time continuum. Who knew the amount of lives that had been altered since he stepped into the Accelerator chamber and began his journey? One altered life altered another, then another, then another, until you had whole generations differing from the ones that might have been . . . *had* been. His thoughts were spiraling out of control, as they did when his excitement or frustration got the better of him. He took a deep breath and let it out in a long, slow stream. Noah Ellman's distorted reflection stared at him morosely from the front of the phone box. He would have to wait for Al to return to give him some clue what his next move should be. Between the two of them they would figure out how to proceed without causing some monumental wound in history.

CHAPTER TWENTY-TWO

A vision floated out of the house, a vision of such ravishing beauty, Al almost choked on his cigar. He froze, one foot on the bottom step, and just . . . stared. The vision was dressed in filmy lime green pants and a matching blouse. "Dressed" was not the right word though. The clothing flowed over her, like gentle waves on clear green Bermudian waters. Barefoot, she wore an emerald ring on her right toe, which to Al was the best part of the package. Something about it made his mouth go dry. And her face was perfect, like a porcelain doll's. The corners of her tiny mouth curled down in a question, those long-lashed blue eyes taking him in. Her blond hair flowed over her shoulders, then down to caress the tops of her breasts.

“Can I help you?”

Al reached down deep inside to regain his composure and pull out some of that Calavicci charm. Removing the cigar from between his teeth, he smiled. “I'm sure you can, sweetheart.”

“Ooh, hey, is that your Ferrari with the cracked windshield?”

“As a matter of fact, it is.”

“I can see you've been greeted officially by Eddie. He takes it upon himself to offer a bit of old-fashioned hospitality to the out-of-town guests.” She placed a delicate finger to her lips and clicked her tongue. “I guess I should have another talk with him. He's going to scare away all my customers.”

“Your . . . customers?” The light blazed on like a supernova.

“Step right in.” She swirled her hips seductively.

This is a bordello! Gooshie's holed up in a house of . . . sin.

It was too funny. Al bit back his laughter. “I'm not here for . . . that. At least not right now,” he added quickly. “Actually, I'm looking for someone I know.”

She shrugged, causing a delicious shift of her blouse. “Can't help you then.”

“Sure you can, honey. I'm here to see Gooshie. Irving Gushman. Just please tell him the admiral is here to see him.”

“Ooh, the admiral. That's pretty ginchy.” She winked.

“Then you'll get him?”

She licked her lips, which caused Al's heart to flutter like hummingbird wings. “No can do,” she sang.

He took one step up, then another. “Look, sis. I work for the government and I'm here on official business.” He reached for his wallet in his back pocket, but froze when he found himself looking down the barrel of a Derringer.

"You'd better leave now. Admiral."

"Let me see the madam." He was shouting now. Gun or no gun, he wasn't leaving until he got what he came for.

"You got her."

"You?"

"I'm afraid so."

"You're too young."

"Thank you, but looks can be deceiving. Now, are you going or do I have to leave you with a souvenir neither you or your girlfriend will appreciate?" She aimed the pistol a few inches lower.

"Gooshie!" he shouted. "Get out here now!"

"Hey!" she said. "Quit yelling. You're not in some barrio, y'know."

Setting his laptop down, Al placed his hands on his hips and glared at her. "Listen, sis, I know people who could shut you down in the time it takes to twitch your pretty little hips."

She smirked. "Yeah, and they're probably all here, enjoying the fine services we provide."

"Dammit, Gooshie!" He staggered back off the steps and squinted up at the second-floor windows.

"Admiral?" Gooshie stumbled around from the side of the house. "Is that you?" His face was beet red, his hair stuck out in all directions, looking as if it hadn't been combed since he left the complex. He wore a pair of orange bathing trunks and a Mickey Mouse T-shirt. Clutched in one hand was a bottle of Jim Beam. "See?" he shouted to the madam. "What did I tell you? I knew it. I *knew* it." He sank to the ground, cradling the bottle to his chest as if it were a newborn. A few tearless sobs shook him as he rocked to and fro.

The madam drifted down the steps, tucking the pistol

between the folds of her blouse. She tossed Al a gorgeous glower, rolling her hips as she moved toward Gooshie. She sat beside him, taking a swig from the bottle when he offered, then stroked his cheeks and hair.

"Did you go in the pool, sweetie?"

"No." He tilted his head, pouting.

"You should cool off. You're so-o-o sweaty and hot."

And drunk.

"What the hell?" Al shook his head in quiet amazement.

They sat that way, conversing in murmurs and whispers, for what seemed a long time. Occasionally the madam would glance at Al, furrowing her lovely brow in disdain, then turn back to Gooshie, finding her smile.

Finally she floated off the dirt, bearing no mark of the dust and debris in which she had just sat, and approached Al. "He'll talk to you. But when he tells you to leave, you'd better listen, or I'll know about it and so will Yancy." She fingered the approximate vicinity where the gun resided, then drifted up the stairs.

"Another time," Al whispered longingly. He yanked his gaze from her retreating hips and made his way toward Gooshie.

CHAPTER TWENTY-THREE

"You're late."

"I know."

"I hope you have a good reason."

"I do."

Sam quickly settled himself behind his desk. The majority of paperwork from yesterday had been packed in boxes behind his chair. The work that would take up much of his time today was spread out into four moderately sized piles before him.

"I have a friend who I think is going to make a poor judgment call, a bad life decision. I stopped at a pay phone to call him, but then I decided not to. At least not yet.''

''Why?'' She sat on the edge of the desk. The stern boss-lady veneer she'd affected when he arrived was dissolving.

''It's kind of a delicate matter. I need to talk to another friend—my best friend, actually—for some advice on how to proceed.''

''So this best friend is someone you can depend on?'' Her face seemed paler than the day before, the shadows beneath her eyes more prominent. She crossed her arms as if to draw comfort from her own embrace. She seemed so emotionally fragile—like a delicate piece of china that could break with the slightest provocation. *Why?* He wanted to get her talking. Perhaps if he put her at ease she would open up to him . . .

''Yes.'' Sam nodded, studying her with concern. ''He's one of the only people I can trust implicity.''

''What about your mom?''

''Uh . . . her too.''

''Then you're very lucky, having two people in your life you can rely on. Don't ever take that for granted.'' She slipped off the desk and made her way to the piano. ''It's going to be a little quieter today than yesterday. Two cancellations—a sore throat and a family emergency. I figured we could use the time to run through some accompaniments I may need you to do.'' She sat on the bench. ''You mentioned at the interview you read music.''

''Yeah, that's no problem.'' Fortunately, his past musical experiences were ones he could recall without being stymied by the Swiss-cheese holes in his memory. He remembered the thrill of playing the Beethoven *Pathetique* Piano Sonata at Carnegie Hall when he was only sixteen, and how music had been a source of comfort when his father died. Then there was Nicole. How sweet his Leap reunion with his childhood music teacher had been (even though to her he had been her long-lost love from Juilliard). Sam rested his head on his hands, grateful to God Time Fate or Whoever for allowing him to remember this much . . .

"Well?" Rebecca's eyes were round with impatience.

"Huh?"

"I'm waiting for you, and all you can do is sit there grinning to yourself."

"I'm sorry." He pushed out of his chair, then started across the room, but the bottom corner of the desk hampered his progress, catching on the hem of his pants. He stumbled forward, twisting his leg in an attempt to keep his balance and not rip the fabric. He failed on both counts, collapsing in a heap between the desk and a cactus plant, and tearing a small, ragged hole in his pants leg.

Oh boy . . .

Rebecca's laughter filled the room. In his attempt to stand, Sam grabbed hold of the closest object available—which just happened to be the cactus. He yelped, scratching his palm on its spiny protrusions.

Rebecca laughed harder, hurrying to his aid. "Can't take you anywhere," she said, gripping his upper arm and helping him up.

"No," he said, joining in her laughter, leaning against her for balance. "Guess you can't."

"Are you okay? Did you hurt yourself?" Opening his hand, she scrutinized the thin scratch on his palm, where blood had beaded up. She dug a tissue from her jeans pocket and held it on the wound. "I can't fix the pants. You're probably going to have to toss those. But I can do something about this. Make a fist."

"No, it's no big deal, really."

"Make. A. Fist."

Rolling his eyes, Sam obeyed.

"Don't roll your eyes. I don't need you getting an infection and applying for workmen's comp the second day on the job.'' Still chuckling, she kneeled to straighten the fallen cactus. ''If you had to be a clutz, you've come to the right place.'' She stood, opening her palms, revealing two bandages across each one. ''We must be compadres.''

''Wow. What happened?''

''Same thing. Almost. I was cleaning behind the cactus, and when I went to push it back in place, I grabbed it instead of the pot. Maybe it's possessed, bending our minds to do its bidding.'' Shrugging, she whistled ''The Twilight Zone'' theme and took Sam by his unhurt hand, ''Come on. Let's wash that off.''

She led him down a corridor lined on either side with framed photographs and magazine articles.

''You had something to do with these, I guess,'' Sam said.

''Every one.'' She stopped to stare at the array, as if she hadn't savored the fruits of her labors for some time.

''It's quite an impressive collection of talent.''

''I'm proud of all of these kids. I feel like, in a way, a little part of their souls will always belong to me.'' She turned to him, her expression difficult to read. She looked at once happy and sad. ''Can you understand that?''

''I think I can,'' he replied, thinking of all the souls he had ''owned'' a piece of for a short span of time. He pointed to a photo of a little girl with curly red hair, emoting in the spotlight. ''Who's this?''

''That's Merrilee Dawbs. She was one of my first students. I've been teaching her for about five years now.''

''She doesn't look much more than nine or ten.''

''Actually, she'll be nine next week. Her mother signed her up the week Merrilee made the transition from training pants to big girl panties.''

Sam laughed. ''Merrilee told you that at the time, I'll bet.''

''It was the major announcement of the day, as I recall.'' Rebecca brushed her fingers along the edge of the silver frame. ''She understudied the roll of Annie on Broadway not too long ago, and actually got a chance to perform. I think no matter what else comes her way professionally, she'll never forget the excitement of her debut.''

''That's great. How'd she do?''

''I . . . heard she was wonderful.'' Her smile faded. ''Come on.''

He followed her down another corridor to the right. *Why didn't you attend the debut performance of one of your most promising pupils?* he ached to ask her. Maybe there was a simple reason, like illness or a prior engagement. The way she felt about these kids, you'd think nothing would have stopped her from going. Maybe she had no choice in the matter, Sam thought grimly, the alarm bells once again waning in his head.

Rebecca snapped on the bathroom light and ran the water in the sink. ''Sit,'' she said, indicating the closed toilet seat. He obeyed, studying the dizzy pattern of treble clefs, half notes and whole notes decorating the shower curtain.

''How's your mom?'' she asked.

''She's great.''

''Getting ready for her audition?''

''Oh.'' He chuffed out a laugh. ''She told you about it?''

''We had some great conversations waiting for you to get your act together. When is it?''

''The day after tomorrow.''

''Bring her over. Maybe I can give her some last-minute pointers or vocal exercises.'' She ran a washcloth under the water, then swabbed it with soap before wringing it out.

On the counter were boxes of bandages and cotton and a tube of antibacterial cream.

He threw her a surprised look. "That's really nice of you, but you might be sorry you offered."

"Why?"

"Because once she starts singing, you might not get her to stop."

"That's okay. I could do with some free entertainment. Your palm, please."

He decided to allow himself to enjoy her ministrations, even with Gooshie in the back of his thoughts. The washcloth felt so cool against his hand as she dabbed at the drying blood. She wiped the excess moisture away with a cottonball. When Al arrives, he thought, delighting in how she looked pursing her lips in concentration as she worked, there will be time enough to finish what has to be done. He could look forward to a truckload of *agita*, and a whole lot of racing against the clock. But at this moment, Rebecca Wexler was caring for his wounds, and he would be damned if he wasn't going to savor every last second of her attentions. He permitted himself to smile and breathe in the wonderful scent of her hair, as her gentle fingers smoothed the ointment over his palm, then placed a bandage over his wound. He was surprised to find her hand lingering inside of his after she was done.

"Thank you." He let his fingers close around hers, which were still damp from the washcloth.

"It was no problem." In one quick, smooth motion, she slipped her hand from his, then busied herself cleaning up the bandage wrappers and collecting the rest of the first aid supplies. "Why don't you head back into the living room and look over some of the sheet music on top of the piano? I'll join you in a couple of minutes."

"Yeah, sure." He clenched and unclenched his hurt hand.

"You think you'll be able to play or should we wait on this?"

"Oh, no," he said, ignoring the sting in his palm. "I'll be okay."

"Good. Start on 'My Funny Valentine,' if you can find it in that mess."

He made it to the doorway before turning to her again. "Do you feel okay?"

"I'm fine," she said quickly, hanging the towel over the shower to dry. "Now, go earn your paycheck."

Maybe he wasn't here for her at all, he thought, heading back toward the living room. He paused at the photo gallery again and could almost hear her students singing her praises. Maybe Al was right. Maybe Sam Beckett couldn't save the world. His jaw tightened as he glanced back toward the bathroom. But what was the point of Leaping if he couldn't try?

CHAPTER TWENTY-FOUR

Al didn't know why he had rolled his cream-colored trousers up just past his knees. Their seat was already saturated with the dusty dirt. A little more on the legs and cuffs certainly wasn't going to irk him any more than he was already irked. But old habits never dic, in his case. He hugged his bare knees and glowered at the mess of a man next to him. The programmer continued to rock himself, continued to take small swigs from his bottle.

"Are you gonna tell me what's up or are we gonna sit here like kids in a sandbox?"

"What's there to say?" Gooshie whined. "You already know. I can't keep anything to myself. Ziggy has more smarts than you give her credit for.'' He blubbered and scrubbed at one bleary eye with his fist.

Al glanced at his laptop, which the madam had agreed to let him set on the steps, out of dirt's way. He should get it, have Gooshie do his thing, then get the hell out of here.

''She's just amazing, isn't she? I mean there were no records to speak of for that silly show, but she found out, didn't she?'' His bloodshot eyes held Al in their inebriated thrall.

''Show? Oh yeah. I mean, we were all . . . taken by surprise.'' Al's stomach clenched, forgetting the laptop for the moment. In his state of drunken melancholia, Gooshie was about to spill something. Al suddenly felt he was teetering on the edge. One wrong word and phffft he would ruin everything.

Gooshie mumbled an unintelligible complaint and put his lips to the Jim Beam. Nothing good would come from its solace, Al knew from his own bout with the bottle years ago. And the liquor did nothing to cover up Gooshie's raging halitosis. If anything, it aggravated it. It was time to say bye-bye, Mr. Beam. Al hitched a breath through his mouth, then reached over to grab the bottle, causing Gooshie to sputter and glare at him. ''Hands off . . . sir.''

''You don't really need this. Not when we're having such a nice chat.'' He sure as hell didn't want Gooshie passing out on him. Not now. ''I'll hold on to it for you.'' Al patted the dirt at his side. ''Ri-ight here.'' Gooshie watched closely as Al capped the bottle and laid it next to him, like precious cargo. ''See? All safe and sound.''

''Hmmph.''

''Please, Gooshie, go on . . .''

Gooshie pouted. ''How did she do it?''

''What?''

''How did she find out I was Marty?''

"Ooooh." *Ooooh boy. "You're* Marty? Heh, heh. Ah . . . that's right, you sure as hell are . . . were."

"How'd she do it?" Gooshie blinked at him.

"I . . ." *Ai yi yi.* ". . . guess she investigated every possible scenario and came up with the answer."

Gooshie rubbed two fingers over his stubbled chin and shook his head. "I didn't wanna do that to Gerda, you know? She was really a great lady. And wha' a dancer. Wow. I was finishin' up my graduate studies at NYU then. My course load was pretty tough, and to take the pressure off at night, I'd go dancin' at the Starlight Ballroom. I always loved to dance. Took lessons as a teenager. It didn't win me any friends but I found out I was good at it." He drew an uneven star in the dirt with his finger. "I met Gerda the first night and something clicked, y'know. She was so different from me, joking around, looking for the silver lining in everything. I was smitten from the start and I think she was too." He chuckled, his eyes misting with the memory. "She roped me into signing up to audition for that contest. After rehearsing with her, I knew if I hung around her any longer I wouldn't be able to leave. That's when I ran." He rubbed out the star with his palm. "I'll bet you didn't know I danced, Mr. Admiral Al Calavicci . . . sir."

"No. I can't say I—"

"I loved that woman." Tears welled in his eyes again.

"She was a lot older than you, wasn't she?" Al said softly.

"Yes." Gooshie's voice was hardly a whisper.

"And that scared you."

Gooshie nodded.

"More than anything, you were afraid of nurturing a special relationship, then having Gerda die on you."

The programmer hung his head; his silence was the only

answer Al needed. Gooshie hitched in a deep breath and let it out slowly. "That's what's good about Ziggy. I can make her better when she's sick."

"Who says you would have lost Gerda? She only died out of disappoint—"

"'Scuse me." Gooshie managed to stand, his balance precarious. He half staggered, half ran to the side of the house and retched in a garbage can.

The combination of the heat, the sounds of Gooshie's regurgitation and the hideous stench hovering over him threatened to work their magic on Al as well. He pulled a cigar from his shirt pocket and lit it, fighting back the swirl of nausea. As an afterthought, he fished out a handkerchief from his pants, and handed it to Gooshie when he returned. "You were saying?"

"I don't wanna talk about Gerda anymore." He sagged to the dirt like a broken jack-in-the-box clown and groaned, clutching the handkerchief Al offered. "How'd you find me?" After wiping his mouth and chin, he offered Al his odorific handkerchief back.

"Uh . . . no, thanks." Al winced, taking a deep pull on his stogie.

"Did you put a tracking device in my suitcase?" Gooshie crumpled the handkerchief, then winged it over his shoulder.

"Yeah."

"You're good. Real good." He placed his mouth against his knees, shoulders heaving as he let out a raspy giggle. "You know what I wish?"

"What?"

"I wish that Sam would fail this time. I wish, I wish, I wish." He closed his eyes and threw his head back, repeating his mantra over and over.

"That's not fair, Gooshie."

"Why not? It's my life you're tampering with. I don' want you to."

"Yeah, well, I guess somebody else does, if you know what I mean." Al gazed heavenward before meeting Gooshie's heavy-lidded stare again.

They sat in silence for a few minutes. From the back of the house came sounds of splashes and giggles and the clinking of glasses. "Someone's having a party," Al said.

"Someone's always having a party here."

"What the hell are you doing in this place, Gooshie? You don't belong here."

"Why the heck not?" The programmer's eyes grew even wider than usual, giving him a zombie-like look. "Oh, I know what you're thinkin' but it's not that way at all, at all."

The madam's toe emerald glinted in Al's mind's eye. He cleared his throat. "The women here—"

"—are my friends. I found them last time you made me take vacation. They give me sanctuary, and I pay 'em for their hospitality. Nothing more."

"Nothing?"

"Nope."

Al shook his head slowly. "Then you never—"

Gooshie's mouth twisted as he pulled on the end of his mustache. "A gentleman doesn't speak of such things."

"You *dog*!" Al stewed for a few moments. A tryst between Gooshie and the picture of loveliness who ran this place was hard to imagine. Al refused to let himself try. "Ziggy would be quite jealous to know you were here."

Gooshie scratched his knee and pouted.

"In fact, she was so upset when you left, she went on strike."

Struggling to his feet, Gooshie staggered toward the laptop, his shoes puffing up dirt. "I gotta talk to her." He sat hard on the bottom step, holding his head in his hands for a moment, then set the computer on his lap. He clicked it open and pressed a few keys to set up the cellular modem connection. Once he was on-line, he typed for a long time, his inebriation abating as he became more absorbed in conversation with Ziggy.

"Admiral, the strike is over," he announced when he was done.

"What did you say to her?" Al looked at him warily.

"I just told her . . ." He looked down at his hands still on the keys, then back to the admiral. "I just told her she was being foolish, and that I would never abandon her."

Al tapped a forefinger to his lips. "That's what she thought, that you weren't coming back, huh?" *Verbeena was right, of course.*

Gooshie's reply was to close the laptop and hold it out to Al.

"Nah. You keep it in case she gets irritable again." He pulled down his trouser legs, then approached Gooshie, one hand outstretched. "Enjoy the rest of your time here. I know I would. And uh, tell Madam maybe I'll see her again sometime."

Gooshie shook his hand. "Thanks, Admiral."

Al started for his car, then turned. "I hope you understand about this Leap, Gooshie."

The programmer had returned to his place in the dirt, and picked up his bottle. He looked haggard but Al could tell he was sobering by degrees. He would have one hell of a headache in the morning, though. "Yeah. But I hope you understand if I don't wish you luck."

"Yeah, Gooshie. I do." He continued walking toward his car. Once inside, he turned on the ignition, leaned back against the seat and basked in the air-conditioned coolness. He couldn't have counted on his luck being this good, and would never have expected Gooshie to blurt out the key to completing the Leap. It had been the booze talkin' and for once it made a whole lot of sense. The Leap wouldn't be smooth sailing from here, but the waters certainly weren't as murky as they had been.

He placed the Ferrari in gear and drove off, not entirely comfortable with his growing optimism. They could still fix things. It was just a matter of Sam getting to Gooshie and convincing him to show up to the audition. Yes, everything would work out. Gooshie might even be better off in the end.

He was rumbling through the heart of town when something popped in his left rear tire. The car thumped and bumped like an ancient heap before Al put on the brake. "What the hell?" He gritted his teeth and got out to investigate. It didn't take long to find the two nails embedded in the tire. He punched the ground, then dug in his pocket for his trunk key. Thank God, Time, Fate or Whoever for giving him the foresight to replace the spare he had used a year ago. He was also glad he'd thought of bringing the cooler of bottled water at the last minute.

He lifted the trunk, then opened the cooler and downed half a liter of Poland Spring before grabbing the jack and getting to work. It might have been the heat, it might have been his mind playing tricks on him as he jacked up the rear of the car, but for a moment he could swear he heard the Wicked Witch of the West's cackle echoing down the deserted street.

CHAPTER TWENTY-FIVE

You could tell volumes about a person by how well they took to their musical accompanist. Some singers liked to lead the music, forcing their accompanist to shift his rhythm to suit them. But Rebecca was happy to work along with Sam. She was an accompanist's dream, holding back slightly to see where he might take the melody, before joining in and giving it everything she had.

He hardly needed to glance at the sheet music for "My Funny Valentine." It turned out to be a song he recognized from somewhere in his convoluted past, and his fingers knew where to go. For this he was grateful, since it allowed him to be an audience as well.

The song might have been written for Rebecca. The ease

in which she melted into the verses, the naturalness of her phrasing suggested she had sung this many times before. The song had special meaning to her. He could tell by the longing in her eyes as she put across the plaintive lyrics. He didn't think she was aware of how much of her inner self she revealed as she sang—he could feel her loneliness, her loss, her overall pain. *Why are you so brokenhearted?* he ached to ask, but knew he couldn't. Something was troubling her—something leechlike that wouldn't let go . . .

She held the last note a long time, then collapsed next to him on the bench. The song had drained her. A tear trickled down her cheek and Sam couldn't stop himself from brushing it away with his thumb. "You okay?" he asked after a moment.

"You're quite a good musician, stylish but not overbearing." She sniffed, then got up and roamed the room, straightening books and knick-knacks that didn't need straightening. "You'll do fine playing for my kids."

"That song means a lot to you." Sam set his hands on the keys and played the gentle refrain.

"Please . . ." Her voice cracked. She froze in the center of the room, her fingers trembling at the bridge of her nose. "Don't play it anymore."

"I'm sorry." He dropped his hands to his sides, frustrated, wanting more than anything to find words that would comfort her. But before he could, she excused herself and ran into the bathroom. The song had touched a nerve, one so sensitive it brought her to tears. So why had she wanted him to play it in the first place? Perhaps she loved it, sang it when she was alone and never had the reaction she did today. Or perhaps it was something else . . .

He grumbled, striking a dissonant chord, annoyed at himself for dwelling on her problems instead of Gerda's. *Where was Al?* It figured. The time Sam really needed him to be here, he was probably swamped with problems at the project, getting Ziggy back in gear. Sighing, he turned to look out the window , but the heavy curtains were drawn, allowing only a sliver of daylight to play on the arm of the sofa. For the first time Sam noticed how stuffy it was in the room. The ceiling fan didn't help—it merely circulated the warmish air. He didn't think any windows were opened. Perhaps Rebecca needed to keep it this way to maintain a proper temperature for vocalizing. *Do you really believe that?* his inner voice pressed. Shrugging, he undid the top button of his shirt and loosened his tie.

He would just bet Rebecca devoted her entire life to her work, never got out, never kicked back or went to the movies to have some laughs. He knew what that was like. If it wasn't for Al dragging him out twice a week to Giordini's, the cozy Italian restaurant in Alamogordo, during the Project's construction, he probably would have become as pasty-faced and as precarious emotionally as Rebecca. Maybe she didn't like going out. Some people were like that. He was that way during his freshman year of college. Or maybe she wanted to—the thought laid into him like a gut punch—but she couldn't . . .

Lunchtime came, but she refused his invitation to dine at the coffee shop on the corner, claiming she was too busy planning the afternoon's lessons. "You go," she told him. He was glad he did. The fresh air revived him; the burger was delicious. The pay phone in the corner beckoned. He fingered the paper in his shirt pocket, the one with Gooshie's number. Again he went to the phone and almost put the dime in, but his trepidation got the better of him. What was he supposed to say? Or rather what was he not supposed to say?

"Al," he lamented into the receiver. "Where the hell are you?"

The afternoon flew by, Rebecca's students parading in hourly for their appointments. Sam noticed while making his calls, and digging deeper into the paper mountain, that Rebecca's mood had improved considerably. It was being around the kids that did it. Why wasn't she teaching in a music school where she'd have a whole classroom of kids to call her own? She could still give private lessons if she wanted to . . .

The sliver of daylight had shifted to a spot on the rug, and the final student of the day had packed her things and let herself out. The abrupt silence was like heavy fog descending, casting a pall over the room. Rebecca had not moved from the piano bench. Sheet music in hand, she stared at the door, her expression stony, blank.

"She has quite a powerful voice for someone so young," Sam offered.

"Sometimes it's too powerful. I'm trying to teach her more control."

Sam placed the completed applications into a file folder and put it away in the bottom drawer of his desk. Tomorrow, after alphabetizing the papers, he would file them in the metal cabinet against the wall.

"Don't forget to ask your mom to come with you tomorrow," Rebecca said sleepily. "I'd really likc to hear her sing."

"Sure. She'd love that." The silence took hold again. "Rebecca?"

"Hmmm?" Her gaze had not shifted at all.

"Why don't you come with me to the audition the night after tomorrow? Mom would be happy if you did."

"And you wouldn't?" A wisp of a smile graced her lips.

"I would be overjoyed if you would accompany me."

He came out from behind the desk and bowed low.

Her smile broadened as she turned toward him, her laughter filling the room like champagne bubbles. The sheet music fell from her hands to the carpet, but she didn't seem to notice. "We used to dance . . . I used to dance . . . every Saturday night." She rose, holding her arms out to Sam. "Will you dance with me . . . again?"

He stood rooted to the spot, heart beating a fervent tattoo against his ribs. Something was wrong. He could tell from her faraway look, how her eyelids fluttered closed as she drifted close and wrapped her arms around him. "Dance with me."

He swallowed hard, struggling against the wave of longing she inspired. It was so difficult to pull away from tenderness, passion. His hands cupped her face, one thumb tracing the dimple on her chin. *Is it so wrong to want her, to breathe in her scent, to stave off the constant loneliness for the few minutes our dance would last? Of course taking part is a selfish act. Where can this relationship go?* Casting logic to the wind, he leaned in to kiss her. Their lips touched, and it was as if he had fallen inside her dream, drifting with her in a slow-motion dance, humming "My Funny Valentine" as she breathed the melody into his ear. Her eyes were still closed as she found his mouth again, the melody lingering as they kissed. His lips brushed her eyes, her neck, her hair, as her hands traveled a gentle, winding path over his back.

Somehow they were by the door. How wonderful it would be to feel the softness of the early evening air mingling with her caresses. It was as if a silent shroud of fog were lifting them up, carrying them both out into the night. Then they were swaying on the porch, the breeze riffling their hair.

The hiss-thump of the door closing caused her eyes to

jerk open. Still in his arms, she gazed around as if awakening from a deep sleep, seemingly unsure of her surroundings. When the slow realization hit her, when she recognized where she was, she wailed, slapping her hands to her mouth. Sam rubbed his forehead, his jaw going slack, the pure terror in Rebecca's eyes hurtling him back to reality. "What? What is it?" He gripped her shoulders but she wrenched away with such force that he feared she would stagger backward and tumble down the steps. He reached both hands out to steady her, but she bolted beneath them and slammed her body hard against the door. Her hands flailed at the knob, her nails scraping against it in vain repetition; still her fingers could not get a grip on it. "It's not safe, David. Notsafe, notsafe, David. Why the hell did you bring me here?" Her voice bore no trace of her frenzy. It was calm, only somewhat argumentative. This must be the way she sometimes talked to—

David . . .

"Here. Wait." Sam clasped her hand, attempting to ease it away from the knob so he could turn it. But her fingers rebelled, stiffening around it like a claw. She dragged in her breaths so hard Sam was fearful she would hyperventilate. His tone was soothing as he murmured inanities meant to calm her, but his words only succeeded in causing her struggle to intensify. Finally his hand managed to tighten over hers, and together they twisted the knob. She fell into the house, moaning, clutching her chest, her face paste white with fear and pain. He took three long strides toward her as she doubled over onto the sofa. "Rebecca."

"Please . . . go . . . home, Noah . . . ," she managed to say between tortured gasps for air. She continued to clasp her chest, clenching and unclenching her other hand against her knee.

"I can't leave you like this."

"Yes . . . you can. Now, go." She pushed him away with all the strength she could muster, then laid her head back on the cushion and blinked at the ceiling.

"Please . . . tell me."

"I'll . . . fire you . . . I goddamn swear I . . . will. Now, leave!"

Rebecca had no use for him or anyone. Solitude would be her balm now. She needed time to recover alone. When she began what seemed to be a ritual devised to calm herself, Sam knew it was not the first time she'd gone through this. Keeping a tight focus on the ceiling, she murmured to herself over and over in a soothing rhythm. Was it a mantra? A phrase of her own design, used to draw her into a more positive mental state? He was not doing her any good standing here, hands folding and unfolding at his sides, as if his presence could miraculously end her suffering. It didn't matter that his intentions were good. His presence was a hindrance. He felt empty, wrung dry. Al had been right. Sam's true purpose here was to help Gerda not Rebecca Wexler. *You can't save the world, kid.*

With great reluctance, he turned away, taking the long walk back to the door. Pulling it open, he couldn't help turning to look at her again. To his surprise, her eyes were on him.

"I can meet with your mother tomorrow." Her voice was weak, used up. "That is . . . if you still want to work for me."

"Do you still want me to?"

"Yes."

"Then I'll be here—we'll . . . be here." He shut the door softly behind him and tramped down the steps, feeling more than a little frustrated. He had done nothing on this Leap but shuffle papers, make a few phone calls and let his libido get the best of him. He had to make a positive change.

Soon. Now! A few feet ahead was the corner of Flatbush Avenue and Avenue B. A left turn would take him back to Gerda's; a right would lead him to the subway, Greenwich Village and Irving Gushman. He set one foot in front of the other, putting mental miles between his better judgment and his impatience . . . and took a hard right at the corner.

CHAPTER TWENTY-SIX

The rumble of the subway lulled Sam. He sat in a corner seat, stomach full from the two street-vendor hot dogs he'd eaten before boarding the train. He leaned his head against the cool metal wall, continuing to wonder why nothing on this Leap was going right. So far he hadn't come close to rectifying anything he'd set out to do. Gerda's longevity was still on shaky ground; tonight he'd come very close to sending Rebecca to the hospital. The doctor in him had turned her symptoms over and over and come up with a clue as to what her problem might be. But he couldn't be sure of his diagnosis until he ran it by Al and Ziggy. Besides, he had promised himself he wouldn't dwell on Rebecca for a little while. One crisis at a time. *Cast your eyes to the center ring, ladies and gentlemen! You'll see the forthright Leaper overcome all odds to triumph over the tragedy of the hour, and win Gerda back her life.*

Ha. Ha.

The train stopped with a huff, the conductor's metallic voice announcing the Eighth Street station over the speakers. Sam followed the crowd onto the subway platform, then up the stairs, getting a good whiff of exhaust fumes and sweat before even reaching the street.

Eighth Street was bustling with activity. Behind the brightly lit shop windows were items ranging from the exotic to the mundane. Street vendors hawked everything from watches to cameras to Western-style fringe jackets to books, giving the legitimate stores some heavy competition. Hot-dog trucks and salty pretzel carts were doing turn-away business. Sam would have liked to linger, but he couldn't afford a casual stroll. There was no time. He wended his way through groups of pedestrians enjoying one of the last balmy evenings they'd have until spring. Many of the guys wore beards, their hair long and fashionably scruffy; the women had that earth mother look: long straight hair, frayed jeans and Grateful Dead T-shirts. They might as well have been wearing "Death to Disco" signs around their necks. The flash and glitz of this decade were nowhere in evidence. This was a college town: Greenwich Village, Sam learned from a street map he bought in the subway, encompassed the campus of New York University. Recalling bits and pieces of his own college years, he figured these kids thought they breathed rarified air, and would never deign to embrace what the masses adored.

Sam forced his attention to the building numbers, and soon found himself standing in front of 220 West Eighth Street—the Taylor Arms Hotel. It was a highbrow name for a decidedly low-class place. A tattered green-and-white striped awning flapped lethargically in the slight breeze. One side of the glass entranceway was boarded up. Sam eased open the other door and entered the dim, musty lobby, padding over the patchy wine-colored carpet to the desk. It took the clerk a full minute to look up from his racing form. "What can I do for you?" he asked, one tobacco-stained finger holding his place.

"I'm looking for Irving Gushman."

The clerk's unoccupied finger scrawled down the guest list. "Third floor, room three-o-two."

"Thanks," Sam said, but the clerk had already returned to the world of Win, Place and Show.

Sam did a perfunctory search for an elevator. He wasn't surprised not to find one, and bounded up the stairs. The yellowish lights on the landing flickered; the peeling wallpaper was the color of eggplant. If he was hoping for relief from his doldrums, he wouldn't find it here.

The same wine-colored carpet paved the third floor. Here it was marred by cigarette burns and greasy footprints. He wrinkled his nose at the stale smells of old dirt and greasy burgers, and approached room 302. Without hesitation, he rapped on the door, deciding not to plan his spiel. The words would come. He could only hope they'd be the right ones.

He rapped on the door again, hearing only the muted drone of a televison from the room next door. Leaning his ear to the ancient wood got him nothing but a small splinter in his earlobe for his trouble.

"You lookin' for the Gushman?"

He spun around. A woman who could have given Hulk Hogan a good workout glared at him from the across the hallway. She wore denim overalls and a red and black checked shirt. Feet apart, hammy arms akimbo, she took up the entire doorway of her room. "I mean Irv Gushman.

I call him the Gushman, 'cause I think he's kinda cute. You're cute too, but you're too pretty. I don't think a man should be pretty, unless he's a movie star. You ain't a movie star, are you?

"N-no."

"Uh, huh . . ." She continued to give him the evil eye. Lowering his gaze, he knocked on the door again.

"He ain't home. Tonight's his dancing night."

A welcome *whoosh* sounded behind Sam. He whirled around again in time to see the imaging chamber door close behind Al. The hologram plodded out of the light, each step a major effort. He flicked an ash from his cigar, then scratched his stubbled cheek, cringing at the sight across the hall. "Oooh. I see you've finally met the girl of your dreams, Sam."

"The Gushman likes to tango."

"The . . . Gushman?" Al exclaimed.

"He likes to cha-cha-cha." The woman swung her hips, wearing the same bulldog expression. The sight of her moving in rhythm was almost too much for Sam to take. He bit the edge of his lower lip, willing away the bubble of hilarity rising in his throat.

He choked. "Do you know where I might find him?"

She shrugged. "He's probably at Club Air."

"Impossible." Al tapped the link; his jaw dropping as he read the data. "But that's where he is."

"Guess he's havin' one blast for the road, this being his last night in town and all."

Sam threw Al a desperate look, before abruptly switching gears and offering the woman a toothsome grin. "Thanks very much."

"Hey, you don't hafta leave so soon, do you? I got some Johnny Walker, some weenies in the blankets . . ."

Hotfooting it back to the stairs, Sam raised one hand in

farewell. Al kept up the pace, drifting alongside him. "I see you've discovered the identity of our mystery man."

"So did you," Sam hissed. "How—"

"You're nothin' like your friend, you know that? He's *no party poop!"*

Sam ducked into the stairwell, then raced down one flight. He leaned his back against the wall of the landing, half expecting Mad Mountain Dina to come after him with an axe.

"Don't worry, Sam." Al appeared at his side. "She went back in her apartment. I think you disappointed her. She had plans for you . . ." He attempted a sly grin, but only managed a yawn.

"I have enough problems. And what's the matter with you? You look exhausted."

"It's been the day from hell, but never mind that now. Ziggy says your girlfriend upstairs is right; Gooshie is at Club Air, so you might as well forget about talking to him tonight."

"What's so special about Club Air?" Annoyance tinged Sam's tone. "It's like you want to genuflect every time it's mentioned."

"Club Air doesn't usually let in schleps like Gooshie. Ziggy says he goes to school with the son of the owner—saved the old man a bundle when he did his taxes. Now Gooshie's got some sort of gold V.I.P. pass to the place."

"Well, c'mon, let's go—"

"Sa-am, haven't you been listening to me? Read my lips. You are not going to get in."

But Sam was already racing down the remaining steps, glancing over his shoulder a couple of times, making sure Mad Mountain hadn't decided to follow. He reached the lobby, where Al floated by the door.

"Sa-am, you're wasting your time."

There was no pounding of size twelve feet on the stairs; the desk clerk was dozing at his post, nodding over his sure bets.

"Are you coming?" he asked Al.

"Do I have a choice?"

"Not in this lifetime," Sam told him.

They made their way uptown via a combination of subway train and footpower. Al apologized for taking so long arriving, explaining how after changing his flat, he had noticed that his other rear tire had also fallen victim to what was most likely another one of crazy old Eddie's pranks. "Had to call Triple A, then wait for them for an hour. The waiting wasn't too bad though. I sat on the floor in the lobby of this fleabag hotel called the Monte Crisco." He laughed. "They had stacks and stacks of old *Playboy* magazines set up on orange crates in there."

"What were you doing on the floor?"

"Enjoying the many attributes of Miss April of nineteen sixty-two."

"On the floor?"

"Sam, every chair and moth-eaten sofa in the place was occupied by some derelict drooling over a magazine. I felt like I was in the Bowery branch of the New York Public Library."

"Guess you felt right at home." Sam smirked.

"Ha. Ha."

On the train, they exchanged notes on how each one had discovered "Marty's" true identity, and how Sam's fear for the future had initially held him back from approaching Gooshie without first consulting Al.

"It's gonna be tricky, Sam, because you can't mention the Project or anyone involved in it at all. It's tempting, I know. I mean, you could tell him who you are, what you did, maybe fix it so you wouldn't take that first Leap. But that information in itself could jeopardize the Project's inception and Gooshie's involvement in it.'' He was silent for a moment. ''I don't know if anyone could handle Ziggy the way he does. He convinced her to call off the strike.''

''How?''

''Oh, by spewing out the usual sweet talk, vowing eternal devotion and all that.''

Sam couldn't help chuckling as Al told him about the madam making nice to Gooshie outside the brothel.

''It wasn't funny.'' Al pouted.

''I'd say it was good for some comic relief.'' Sam rubbed his eyes, then blinked at the half-empty car, grateful they could talk freely here. A man babbling to himself on a New York City subway train was not considered out of the ordinary. No one even glanced his way.

''You look like *you* could use some comic relief, Sam.'' Al scrutinized him for the first time since he'd returned. ''What's the problem?''

Sam gave Al a troubled look.

''Is it Gerda?''

''It's Rebecca Wexler.''

The link squealed as Al rolled his eyes. ''I told you, Sam—''

''I know what you told me, Al. But I can't ignore what happened tonight.''

''What?''

Sam sighed and looked down at his hands. ''Has Rebecca taken any trips in the past year or so?''

The link chattered, its lights dancing as Al poked its keys for data. ''Nope.''

''How about over the past eighteen months?''

Ziggy squealed. ''Nope.''

''When was the last time she went anywhere?''

"Ahhh, let's see. Oh, here we go. February, 1976, Rebecca Wexler traveled to Aspen, Colorado, for a vacation with a guy named David Cullen."

David . . . why the hell did you bring me here?

"They stayed for a week, then returned home to Brooklyn."

"Nothing since?" Sam tapped one finger on the armrest.

"Nada."

"Who's David?"

"Fiancé. Oops, late fiancé. He died not long after that Aspen trip."

Sam turned to him slowly, the alarm in his head wailing like a trio of firetrucks. "How?"

"Gunshot wound to the chest. He got caught by a stray bullet. Two rocket scientists decided to have a very volatile 'conversation' on the Flatbush Avenue subway platform, and I guess David got in the way."

The wheels clicked in Sam's head, the puzzle pieces falling into place . . . "Al, I think the trauma might have caused Rebecca to become agoraphobic."

The Observer groaned. "Sam, just because she hasn't taken a trip in a while doesn't mean—"

Pounding his thigh, Sam leaned into Al's face and hissed, "Dammit, Al. She's afraid to leave her house. She almost had a heart attack tonight when she stepped out onto the porch."

The train screeched to a stop. A few weary-looking passengers boarded, seating themselves as the doors slid shut. With two short huffs, the train was moving again.

"I understand your concern for this woman Sam, but Ziggy says . . ." Al brought the link closer, narrowing his eyes at it suspiciously.

"What?" Sam strained to read the green crawl line.

"She says the chance that you're here for Rebecca as

well as Gerda has jumped from forty-two point four to seventy-six point nine percent over the past five hours." He looked at his friend with renewed respect.

"Sometimes I'm right." Sam crossed his arms and hitched up his brows.

"Yeah, sometimes you sure as hell are."

CHAPTER TWENTY-SEVEN

When Sam was twelve years old, he developed a fascination for New York. His friend Joey had sung its praises after vacationing there, chattering for weeks about the buildings, the shows—everything! In Sam's fanciful imaginings, it was a city inhabited by interesting, complex people, whose heads were filled with editorials from the *New York Times* and stock market prices from the *Wall Street Journal*. They worked in luxurious offices inside imposing glass and steel skyscrapers, making decisions affecting everyone's life—even an intellectually advanced farmboy's in Elkridge, Indiana. Now he wondered what twelve-year-old Sam Beckett might have thought of the "interesting, complex" New Yorker on the corner, screeching in an off-key falsetto about a "candy girl," while jumping like some jungle beast around a battered cowboy hat. Stubborn young Sam, refusing to have his bubble burst, might have reasoned that the guy was just a visitor to the fair city. The older, wiser Sam snorted, knowing better. He tossed a quarter in the cowboy hat before crossing the street with Al.

"Now, I'm telling you, Sam, you're wasting your time. Just look at those nozzles waiting behind the police barricades on Fifty-second Street over there."

Across the next intersection, the red and gold "Club Air" sign glittered atop the jet black building, as the commotion of an "event" ensued. Paparazzi hovered by the club's entrance, hoping to get a coveted shot of someone much loftier than the "ordinary extraordinaries" behind the barricades. Those "extraordinaries" were dressed in their finest glitter and glitz, in open shirts and heavy gold chains. Some had purple hair, others were in whiteface. None wore smiles.

"They look like they want to go home," Sam said.

"They've been waiting here for hours and probably do, but they can't without at least trying to get in. The guys at the door walk down the line two or three times a night, bestowing that privilege on a couple of people they think are the hippest, the freakiest, whatever."

Sam gave his dress shirt, his beige trousers and Hush Puppies a morose once-over, then met the amused eyes of the hologram. "I don't have a snowball's chance, do I?"

"No. You don't. You should have saved yourself a token and gone back to Gerda's." Al clicked his tongue against his teeth as he eyed the crowd. "Wait here. I'm going to see what Gooshie could possibly be up to in there." He pressed three buttons on the link and was gone.

• • •

The disco era held no charm for Sam. He detested it. But Al was quite happy to have been thrust into the decade of platform shoes and mood rings. It was so mindless, so glittery, so different from the hellish, war-torn years that had preceded it. After Al was repatriated from Vietnam, he was open to mindless diversions—especially ones involving scantily clad young women swaying their hips and shakin' their booties to seductive rhythms. Club Air had plenty of those. Al lit up a Havana, blew out a stream of smoke and strutted through their midst as they gyrated with their partners on the packed dance floor. Satin shimmied against satin in this land of platform-shoed giants. Diamonds glinted on fingers and around necks, reflecting in Gucci shades. Donna Summer's "Love to Love You, Baby" groaned and moaned through the massive speakers on the domed ceiling.

Al rolled his hips and shoulders, singing a bit of the erotically charged refrain as he moved on. Gooshie was nowhere in this crowd, but private rooms abounded in exclusive clubs like these. He had frequented enough of them to know. Gooshie could be . . . involved in the old horizontal cha cha cha, in which case Al would take quick flight. He had no desire to witness even one moment of Gooshie's sex life.

He made his way past the dance floor, down a flight of Day-Glo blue stairs and discovered a private bar. A lanky blond man wearing glittering white overalls and no shirt was checking passes of the few that sought entrance. Al drifted through the smoked glass door into the purplish light of the room. The carpet was mulberry, thick enough to sink into, if you weren't a hologram. The bar was L-shaped, taking up half the room. The rest of the barroom was set aside for dancing—a small mirror ball swirled above a square parquet floor and Chuck Mangione's "Feels So Good" throbbed at a moderate volume from the ceiling. Right now the privileged patrons preferred imbibing to rug cutting. A few nursed their drinks at the bar, chatting with one another and the bartender; some had drifted to private tables lining the walls. One couple was seated on a long leather sofa adjacent to the tables. The guy was sobbing into his Scotch, the doll cooing in his ear. Al frowned: the sobs sounding familiar, too familiar.

"Gooshie!"

If he hadn't been on the hunt for him, Al wouldn't have recognized this nebbish in the tan leisure suit and platform shoes.

Al paced, narrowing his eyes in scrutiny. "You look better without the mustache, you know that?"

Their eyes met. Gooshie swayed into the woman's skinny shoulder, blinked twice then downed the rest of his drink. The inebriated, the slow-witted and the very young were among those who could detect Al's presence. But maybe this was not the time to take advantage of that fact. Gooshie was not in the best shape to follow a logical train of thought.

He was prattling to his empty scotch glass. The woman leaned closer to hear what he was saying, then looked in Al's direction, shaking her head.

Aw, what the hell. "Gushman, this is your conscience speaking." Al's voice boomed. "I'm not hangin' around here for my health."

Gooshie's saucer-wide eyes expanded to the size of serving platters.

"You don't show up to that audition, you're gonna regret it."

Gooshie moaned and let his glass fall to the carpet.

"Whatsamatta now, baby?" The woman pouted, her

eyes glazing over. Al could tell she was growing tired of playing mommy. It wouldn't be long before she moved on, ruining Gooshie's night. This was good.

"Think about it." Al chomped on his cigar and turned his back on Gooshie, not wanting the programmer to catch a glimpse of the handlink before his time. Snickering with wicked glee, Al centered himself back on Sam.

More of the "ordinary extraordinaries" had come to roost behind the barricade. The queue was now almost to the corner. "Don't they see the futility of it?" Sam sat on the curb, elbows on knees, chin cupped in his hands. He looked downtrodden, like a puppy kicked out into the cold. "I mean, why do they even bother?"

Al smirked. "It's important to make the scene, to say you were here. That in itself is a badge of honor."

"It's stupid." Sam stood and brushed off the back of his trousers.

"You tried, didn't you?" Al said, cigar clamped between his teeth.

Jabbing his hands in his pockets, Sam hitched up his shoulders and tramped back in the direction of the subway.

"Didn't you?"

"They laughed at me." He spoke to the ground. "The guy at the door said nobody believed the Pacino face and to 'get real' "

"Don't feel too bad, Sam. You couldn't have done much, even if you'd gotten inside."

"Why not? Isn't Gooshie in there?"

"Yeah, but he's blitzed—babbling and crying, looking like he did in Verdad." Al referred to the link. "You'll have to get to him tomorrow. Ziggy says the best time to snag him is on his lunch break. She's accessed his schedule, which has him taking a couple of classes in the morning—advanced computer science at nine-ten, physics from ten-thirty till noon. And at one-ten he's got advanced calculus. You've gotta get to him right after physics."

"How am I going to do this, Al? I have to go to work." Sam shook his head. "Why isn't anything working out?"

"Have Gerda fill in for you for a few hours."

The knot in Sam's gut eased. The idea had definite possibilities. Straightening his shoulders as they approached the subway entrance, Sam said, "You're a genius, Al. That's the best idea I've heard all day. Rebecca asked to hear her sing tomorrow anyway." He paused at the top of the stairs, one hand resting on the cool metal bannister. "Check on her for me, will you?"

"Gerda?"

"No. Rebecca."

Al pulled the stogie from his mouth, eyeing Sam with concern. "You okay?"

"I'm just worried about her, Al, and sick over the fact I haven't been able to change Gerda's situation at all." An elderly woman brushed past him, then a teenaged boy and a gaggle of nuns. "I don't think I've ever felt so . . . ineffectual."

"Well if it will make you feel better, I'll peek in on Rebecca." He popped out. Sam paced to the curb and back twice in the time it took Al to return.

"How is she?"

"She's fine, Sam. She's propped up in bed, reading, all nice and cozy under her comforter. There's a cup of hot tea on her nightstand. Anything else you want to know?"

"No, Al. Just as long as she's okay." Sam returned to the subway steps, his footsteps echoing as he descended to the cool depths of the station.

"You might be interested to hear that Rebecca was reading a book on panic disorders . . ."

Sam froze on the last step, waiting for the other shoe to drop.

". . . and that the odds are now even at ninety-one point six percent that you're here to help both Gerda Ellman and Rebecca Wexler."

CHAPTER TWENTY-EIGHT

As Rebecca turned the pages, she was surprised by a song popping into her head. Sometimes songs did that; so many of them were stored in her gray matter, occasionally one decided to jump up and give her a nudge. "In My Own Little Corner," from the Rodgers and Hammerstein musical *Cinderella*, was a tune she hadn't thought of in a long time. A student had considered using it for an audition last year, but opted for "Consider Yourself," from *Oliver!* instead.

She set the book down, closing her eyes, trying to recall the words. They had something to do with staying in your own little corner in your own little chair, and being whoever you wanted to be. Well, that sounded like her, didn't it? After what happened earlier, it was no wonder her thoughts had turned to self-comfort and self-preservation.

Opening her eyes, she sighed, allowing herself to sink deeper into her pillows. She turned on her side, then stretched to reach for her cup on the nightstand. Settling back, she held it to her chin, the steam playing on her cheeks and lips. She sipped the strong hot liquid, enjoying how it warmed and soothed her. It was like an old friend come to call, an old friend who wouldn't delve or pry or send her into an emotional tailspin.

Setting her cup on the nightstand, she thought of Noah. Poor guy. It wasn't his fault what happened. Judging by how beaten he looked before he left, it would be hard to convince him of that. From her reading, she had learned that agoraphobics experienced bouts of *derealization*, when time seemed to slow, and everything around them seemed . . . different. Colors might brighten or dim; everyday sounds would mutate into oddly distorted waves. Combined with her intense thoughts of David, brought on by "My Funny Valentine," (she was her own worst enemy, singing the song David crooned to her softly, like a lullaby, after lovemaking), and her attraction to Noah, this had sent her off into her "own little corner"—a time and place of her own imagining. But when that door hissed closed and the outside air brushed her cheeks, she felt she'd been thrust into her own little corner of hell; her heart felt like a cold chip of granite, feebly attempting to pump . . . pump . . . pump to keep her alive. Never had she been so terrified. Even now, lying here in such a safe place, the tips of her fingers tingled, her stomach rumbled and cramped up. She clenched her teeth, willing away the onslaught, the symptoms of her illness. And yes, it was an illness, but it was her secret and would remain that way. Since David died, she had fended for herself quite well, thank you. And she would keep herself together by remaining safe in her thoughts and in her home. That was the key. Safety.

Earlier, she'd received a phone call, which couldn't have come at a worse time. Noah had been gone for a little over an hour, and Rebecca had spent most of that time in the bathroom, fighting off the shakes and the nausea that were common weapons in agoraphobia's artillery. She had just climbed into bed, hugging her comforter to her, when the phone rang.

She waited almost long enough to let the answering machine pick up, but, thinking it might be Noah, she grabbed the receiver from the nightstand in time. It was Gerda. Rebecca was surprised at the sense of relief she felt hearing her confident, slightly raspy voice again. But now that voice was filled with concern. Noah hadn't come home after work and she wondered if Rebecca might know why. Rebecca frowned, not recalling much about the last hour Noah was at the house, except her own pain. She attempted to keep the residual tremor from her voice, saying he probably had some things to do—earlier he had mentioned a friend who was having some problems—perhaps he went to help him out.

They chatted for a long time, longer than Rebecca would have thought possible in her condition. They talked about music, about Gerda's years on the Catskills stage, about Rebecca's college years. She mentioned her family only in passing, and David not at all. She didn't need those memories overtaking her again. Gerda had even managed to make her laugh, which felt extraordinarily good. The ease with which the conversation flowed enabled Rebecca to place the evening's ordeal behind her for a while. And it became obvious, the longer they spoke, how strongly the mother's sensibilities had influenced the son. Gerda's compassion, her sharp sense of humor, even her love of music had been passed along to Noah. Rebecca wondered if he realized how lucky he was to have her.

When she asked to hear Gerda sing tomorrow morning, the invitation was accepted with a barely restrained whoop. "It would mean so much to get your professional input," Gerda said. "And I want you to come with Noah to the audition."

Rebecca choked back her excuse. She didn't want to disappoint this woman in any way tonight. Not after deriving so much comfort from her. Rebecca thanked her quietly, and after they said their good nights, she had stared at the ceiling for a long time.

Her hand rested on the panic disorder book she would soon return to its dark home under the bed. Out of sight, out of mind? Not really. The anticipatory feeling of dread was always there, hovering somewhere over her shoulder, like the hated presence in her dream. Waiting . . . always waiting.

She fell asleep and this time dreamed she had reached her safe spot. It had shrunk to the size of a kitchen tile. All around her black, brackish water rose out of the sands, boxing her in. If she moved an inch this way or that, she would stumble into the water wall and be swallowed up.

Her panic rose in tandem with the wall. Behind her the voice—that hated voice—sniggered, then hissed, "Turn around, Rebecca. Turn and see me."

No! She put every ounce of mental energy into remaining rooted to the spot. But the dream voice compelled her, the waters receding just enough to allow her to turn herself around inches at a time to see . . . her. The woman opened her mouth in a hideous abomination of a welcoming grin. Blackened teeth gleamed, cheekbones jutted through a thin gauze of skin. Her eyes were Rebecca's eyes, deep caverns leading down to the heart of a withering soul. Rebecca felt her own heart pause, then join the thundering pounding of the other. *Finally.* Their fingers entwined as the water rose again, but this time Rebecca was not afraid. She was imprisoned, but her safety was assured. She breathed a sigh of relief, which echoed over and over, rippling the waters. Now she was complete.

CHAPTER TWENTY-NINE

Sam dreamed of prison, of iron bars that grew like Jack's beanstalk up, up into heavy black clouds. He paced his cell, trying to avert his eyes from what was going on just beyond those bars. Rebecca was lying on the ground, reaching for him, shouting for him, her clawlike fingers barely brushing the cold blue steel. Something was pulling her away, into a darkness so fathomless, he knew she would never return once she succumbed to it. Still he paced, silent, unable to help . . . Gerda appeared next to her, her face a clown mask—huge red lips, cherry nose, her red hair a flame that shot sparks into the waiting darkness. She jittered and jerked like a marionette possessed, her dance growing more frantic and frenetic as the moments slipped by. Sam knew she was powerless to stop, but death would come to her aid without much more provocation. He fell to the cold cement floor, hiding his face in his hands, trying to wish away the cries and moans of those he had failed . . .

"Noah."

He struggled to awaken, glad for the hammering of his heart against his ribs reminding him he was still able to affect change.

"Noah, I guess you forgot to set your alarm. In case you didn't notice, daylight, glorious daylight, has arrived and is peeking through your blinds. This is a damn good indication that it's time to get up."

Gerda stood at the foot of his bed, dressed in a lemon yellow pantsuit. Her purse was slung over her arm. Sam pushed his hair back and rubbed his eyes. Where was she going? "Rebecca wants to hear you sing today," he blurted out.

"You think I don't know that?"

"I didn't think—"

"You didn't think I had dinner ready for you last night either when you decided to go gallivanting off to God knows where."

He shrank under her look, which was at once angry and disappointed.

"You're a man, and a man has to gallivant, I know this better than anyone. But please, Noah, next time spare me two seconds of your evening to say, Ma, I got other plans."

"Sorry . . ."

"Feh." She clicked her tongue and took a step back toward the door. "They should make a gold statue of that word 'sorry' and put it in the center of every town. Then people could bring their wives, mothers, husbands, kids, fathers and long-lost cousins there, to sit and worship it."

The metronome beat of her foot tap increased. ''It seems to be everyone's favorite cure-all.''

''I didn't mean—''

''Get up now. I'm ready to go to your job. You should be too.''

Sam pushed off his blankets and got out of bed. ''Did Rebecca call here last night?''

''I called her to see if you were working late.''

''Was she . . . okay?''

Gerda tossed her purse to the floor and moved to the bed as Sam rifled through Noah's middle drawer for underwear. ''She sounded a little tired. But when a person works all day they get tired and usually want to relax.'' She paused, giving him an icy glare. ''Not gallivant.'' She punctuated her annoyance by jab-jab-jabbing the left edge of the sheet under the mattress.

''Sor—er, yeah.'' He said, fumbling through the clothes a bit more desperately, finally coming up with a pair of boxers, a T-shirt and socks. Easing toward the door, he hoped to make it to the bathroom without having to dodge any more barbs.

''No-ah.''

He winced and turned toward her. She was fluffing his pillows, watching him from the corner of her eye. ''I guess I can reheat last night's stew for dinner tonight,'' she said. ''That is, if you're going to show up.''

''I'll be there.'' The stone in his gut shrank to the size of a pebble.

She smoothed the blanket over the bed, then blew out an impatient breath. ''Don't just stand there. We have to get to work.''

''I'm going, I'm going.'' Sam hurried toward the bathroom, a slow smile spreading across his face as he reached the door. Gerda was humming ''Lullaby of Broadway.''

Despite her irritation at him, her spirits were high. He only hoped he'd be able to keep them that way.

Sam approached Rebecca's house, Gerda leading the way. The quick click of her heels contrasted sharply with his reluctant footfalls. ''Why are you moving like you've got lead in your butt, Noah?'' She was already on the porch, while he took the stairs one leaden step at a time. He glanced at the door, afraid of what he might find beyond it.

Gerda's finger was on the doorbell.

''It's open, Mom. Just . . . knock and walk in.''

''That's not safe.'' She rapped softly on the door several times, then twisted the knob. ''Rebecca?'' she called as she stepped inside.

Sam closed the door behind them. ''Rebecca?'' Water was running in the bathroom; a teakettle whistled on the stove. He walked down the hallway to the kitchen, intending to turn off the heat, almost stumbling into Rebecca as she stepped out of the bathroom.

''Noah, I'm sorry. I didn't hear you come in.'' She stood on her toes, straining to see over his shoulder. ''Is your mom here too?''

''Yes.'' He took her hand, which was cold but steady. ''You okay?''

''I'm fine.'' Switching on her heel, she marched into the kitchen and turned off the warbling kettle, Sam following at a moderate clip. The kitchen was the brightest room in the house he had seen so far. The curtains were kelly green, and did a competent job of holding the daylight at bay. But the space between the top and bottom curtains was enough to allow streams of light to shine on the tabletop and a good section of the linoleum. He noticed how carefully she avoided those areas, whenever possible.

''I just thought that after last night—''

''Last night is over.'' She poured hot water into a cup. ''Does your mother like tea?''

Sam hesitated only a moment before saying, ''Sure.''

You're agoraphobic, Rebecca, he wanted to say. *You need help.* How would she react if he did? Would she deny it? Would she become furious? She wouldn't throw him out, not with Gerda in the next room. No, he thought, watching her. The light was like some harsh, unforgiving entity, wrenching away soft shadows, revealing how much thinner and paler Rebecca's face looked today than yesterday. She wore no lipstick, and her lips were one hue shy of being paste white. Now was not the time. She was much too intent on keeping her composure, averting her eyes from his, setting the last of the three cups of tea on a tray that already held a creamer and packets of sugar.

''How is she?'' Al's sudden presence caused Sam to jerk forward, rattling the table.

''Are *you* okay?'' Rebecca asked, giving him a quick look as she lifted the tray.

''Yeah.''

''Bring in those napkins by the side of the sink, please.'' She carried the tea tray out of the room.

Al shifted over to the doorway, watching her go. ''She doesn't look so good, Sam.''

''Tell me about it.'' He sighed, tapping his fingers against the counter. ''She needs professional help, but I get the feeling if I suggest it, she'll snap my head off, Al. It's like she's got something to prove, that she can do everything by herself . . . even though her illness just keeps eating away at her.'' He fingered the napkins, then set them down again and leaned back against the counter.

''Agoraphobia is a physical as well as emotional disease,'' Al said. ''Beeks told me it's caused by a chemical imbalance in the brain brought on, in Rebecca's case, by severe mental trauma. What she needs is medication and therapy."

"How?" Sam lifted his hands, then dropped them in a futile gesture. "How am I supposed to get her to help herself? Maybe a family member could convince her better than me."

Al prodded the link. "Father and brother are archaeologists who spend ten months out of the year in the Middle East."

"What about her mom?"

The link chittered. Al slapped its side, causing it to squeal like a wounded cat. "Dammit, Ziggy."

"What?"

"She's threatening to strike again if I continue to *abuse* her. No, I will not apologize. Do your job, you worn out pile of sprockets." He shook it once, twice, then smirked, triumphant. "Ah, here we go. Rebecca's mother is remarried, living in Seattle. There's no evidence of communication between the two that I can see. No long-distance bills, no plane, train or bus tickets, no gas receipts. They probably don't get along."

"Either that or Rebecca created the gap between them. Maybe it's just another way for her to keep her illness deeply pocketed away." He paused, rubbing his palms together. "Maybe her mother's the key. Maybe we have to get in touch with her—"

"We'll talk about it more on the train."

"Oh boy." Sam checked Noah's watch, then Rebecca's wall clock. It was two minutes to ten. "We've gotta get to NYU."

"Yep."

"And I didn't even tell Rebecca I have to leave." He raced into the music room. Gerda and Rebecca were already seated at the piano, their teacups half-full on the coffee table. Al was already waiting by the door, waving at Sam to hurry up.

"Rebecca, can I talk to you for a minute?"

She stopped in mid-sentence and looked at him over her shoulder. "You forgot the napkins."

"He was talking to himself," Gerda said, playing a soft three-note melody. "I heard you, Noah. You must have money stashed away somewhere. That's what they say about people who talk to themselves."

"I know this is short notice, but . . . remember that friend I told you about yesterday? The one with the problem?"

Gerda leaned closer to Rebecca. "All his friends have problems."

Rebecca giggled. It was a wonderful sound. "Yes, Noah. What about him?"

"Two women together, that's trouble, Sam. You'll never get out of here," Al called.

"I have to go see him today . . . this morning. If I don't, he may do something rash, something he may regret later on."

"What friend is this, Noah?" Gerda asked.

"Uh-oh." Al clicked his tongue. "Here comes the Inquisition. Cut it short."

"Uh . . . you don't know him."

"I know every one of those fine upstanding citizens—"

"Why didn't you tell me about this yesterday?" Rebecca asked.

"That's my son—last-minute Charlie." Gerda moved her three-note symphony up an octave.

"She'd make a great color commentator, Sam."

"I just spoke with him this morning."

"When was this, Noah? I didn't see you use the ph—"

''Would it be all right?'' Sam pressed. He felt like a kid asking his mother for ice cream money.

Rebecca frowned, her gaze drifting to the still-formidable pile of work on his desk.

''I'll fill in for him, Rebecca. If it would help.''

''Oooh, Gerda to the rescue, Sam. Who would have thought . . . ?''

Rebecca looked from mother to son, then back again to Gerda, who was giving her a ''C'mon, let's get the kid the ice cream cone'' look.

''All right. Just don't make a habit of this kind of thing.''

''Bingo!'' Al jabbed a finger at the door. ''Let's get outta here.''

''Thanks, Rebecca. I shouldn't be back later than—''

''Two or three o'clock,'' Al chimed in.

''Oh, two, three o'clock at the latest.''

''*I* didn't hear a thank-you,'' Gerda said, starting on ''Chopsticks.''

''Thanks, Mom.''

''Hmmph. I hope your friend is worth the trouble,'' She smiled as Rebecca played a counterpoint to her melody.

''Yeah, you should only know,'' Sam said under his breath, racing out the door.

CHAPTER THIRTY

Washington Square Park was a gathering place for intellectuals and the everyday working Joe. Sam always felt at home in college towns, having spent a good deal of time in Boston when he attended MIT. College towns were richer and more varied in culture than most, especially when that town was already a demographic melting pot. Here no one was an outcast. The haves consorted with the have-nots. A chess game between a wizened old black man and a tough with a lightning bolt tattoo on his arm was attended by three kids, two nuns, a few people in business dress and a collie who made himself at home at the black man's feet.

Al had accessed some logistical details: surrounding the

park were NYU's Information Center, Student Services Building, Office of Student Life and Career and Health Services, the administrative arteries through which each student had to flow.

Sam seated himself on a bench across from the high stone structure known as Washington Arch. He took a deep whiff of sullied New York air as he savored this brief respite. Al had gone off to see where Gooshie might head after his last class of the morning. The plan was that Sam would then just happen to cross Gooshie's path and hopefully be able to involve him in a conversation. It was an iffy proposition. Gooshie might not want to talk to him. Since he had already decided to leave Gerda in the lurch, her son's appearance would probably not be a welcome surprise. But after tossing around a few other possibilities on the train ride here, they'd settled on this one. Arms crossed, feet tapping along with an edgy inner rhythm, Sam waited.

"We're in luck." Al popped in fifteen minutes later. "He's two blocks away at the Student Services Center, getting the last of the paperwork done for his transfer out to USC. He's carrying a lunch bag. Chances are good he's going to eat after he's done."

Sam got up and fell into step next to Al. "How do you know it's a lunch bag?"

"Typical Gooshie grease stains on the bottom. He must have one hell of a stink-bomb sandwich in there."

They reached 25 West Fourth Street and stood a few feet from the doorway so as not to obstruct the flow of traffic. Sam wondered if the door ever closed completely during the workday. The parade of students and faculty passing in and out was nonstop.

"It's one of the busiest buildings on campus." Al waved his cigar for emphasis. "You got the Offices of the Bursar, Financial Aid and the Registrar in there, Sam. It's also probably a great place to meet women.'' Al gave a long appreciative whistle to a passing brunette wearing a fringed jacket and jeans that might have been painted on. He followed her with his eyes as she crossed the street. ''I think I may go back to school for a while.''

''Al!'' Sam muttered. ''Here he comes.''

Gooshie took two steps out of the building, a grease-spotted brown bag in his left hand, a manila folder overflowing with papers and a physics textbook under his right arm. He stopped in the middle of the sidewalk, looking one way, then the other, as if deciding which way to go, before heading in the direction of the park. Sam gave a slow silent count to twenty before following.

''You know, the thing I don't understand is how much he's changed.'' Al said as they headed back. ''As long as I've known him, Gooshie was never a people person. He eats alone behind that damn console, has meaningful conversations with Ziggy because he enjoys her company more than anyone's with a pulse. But here he's hanging with the disco elite and going to ballrooms, doing the cha-cha.''

''Leaving someone you love changes a person, Al.'' Sam's voice was soft, pensive. ''Something in him died when he decided to never see Gerda again. The hurt and guilt ran much deeper than he'd expected it to.''

They entered the park, keeping their distance as Gooshie passed the chess players and an immense circle in the square where unicyclists offered an impromptu show, then a few student types reading on the grass, a clique of moms wheeling strollers and a derelict sleeping on a bench, utilizing a few rumpled pages of the *New York Times* for a blanket. Sam felt like a bounty hunter moving stealthily after his prey. Had he been a bounty hunter once? Yes—the memories of that Leap came in flashes: handcuffs and a feisty blonde, a barn, hay scratching the nape of his neck, the blonde kicking him into a mud puddle, both of them tumbling into a pile of manure, hating her, *wanting* her, her hair falling over his face as she kissed him. The memory abruptly switched to last night, Rebecca in his arms, his lips moving against the silky softness of her hair . . .

"Heads up!"

A Frisbee landed at his feet. He blinked twice, almost stumbling over his feet as he swam up from his reverie. He retrieved the Frisbee and tossed it to the boy who was running to claim it.

"You're driftin' away on me, Sam."

"I'm sorry, Al." He rubbed his temples, catching sight of Gooshie seating himself on a bench beneath a tree a few feet past Washington Arch. The programmer had chosen a spot well out of range of the Frisbees, moms and chess players. "Looks like he wants to be alone."

"He's probably got a lot on his mind."

Sam slowed his approach, then stopped, his knees like water, his head reeling. He had to sit, rest a minute. He stumbled to a bench, Al was yelling in his ear, leaning into his face, but he waved him away, because suddenly he could *see* Gooshie, *not* Irving Gushman, *his* Gooshie. The memory blasted into him like the heat from an explosion. It was so vivid and strong he had to believe he was being *allowed* to hold it and cherish it like a treasure. Here was the control room, Ziggy's rainbow lights casting shadows over the walls, the console, the blur of techs and others Sam could not quite see. But Gooshie was as clear as crystal. He had been up all night, working out a programming glitch. His eyes were bleary with exhaustion, yet shone with triumph and pride. Sam was shaking his hand, congratulating him on a job well done, all the while keeping a discreet distance because of that terrible breath . . .

"Sam, what the hell's going on with you?"

''Huh?'' The vision melted like ice cream on the sidewalk. He was back in the park. Above him a sparrow twittered. In front of him the hologram eyed him with a mix of concern and impatience.

''Are you gonna sit there all day like a dog with your tongue hangin' out?''

''I remembered . . . ,'' Sam murmured.

''He's on his second sandwich already.'' Al wrinkled his nose at Gooshie in disgust. ''What is that gooey stuff dripping out of the bread? E-yuch.''

''I was just remembering . . .'' Sam looked down at his hands, clasping them together. ''The Project . . . Gooshie . . . the lights.''

''I know, kid.'' Al's voice softened with compassion. ''But you've gotta snap out of it and do what has to be done.''

''I don't want to say the wrong thing.''

''If you just stick to Gerda and the audition, everything will be fine. Now, go.''

If the hologram could have pushed him, Sam knew he would have. Sam forced himself to move off the bench, and affecting a casualness that would have earned him an Academy Award nomination, he strode off toward Gooshie.

''Hi.''

''Mmmph?'' Gooshie started, jerking forward, his open book sliding from his thighs to his knees. He grabbed it just in time to stop it from tilting off his lap, while continuing to chew furiously on the food in his mouth. The brownish secret sauce dribbled off his chin.

''Awfully edgy, isn't he?'' Al twiddled his cigar.

Gooshie placed the book at his side, took a huge gulp of milk from the pint container at his feet, then wiped the goo off his chin. He lifted his submarine sandwich from its wrapping, giving Sam a most unwelcome glare before taking another bite.

"Can I join you?"

Shrugging, Gooshie shifted himself and his belongings to one side of the bench.

"I don't think he recognizes you, Sam."

"I'm Noah, Mr. Gushman. Gerda's son . . ."

He swallowed, his bug eyes growing wider with recognition. "Noah." He smiled, offering his hand. Sam shook it, his tension easing. "You must forgive me. I enjoy eating here, but occasionally I get cornered for spare change or roped into conversation with someone who has too much time on his hands." He picked up his book and found his place. "I don't much care for that. You . . . uh, work around here?"

"No. I just had a few hours off. Thought I'd spend it in one of my favorite parks."

"Mmm." Gooshie turned the page and took another bite of his sandwich. It smelled like garlic, hot peppers and some vile indefinable type of meat.

The silence and the sandwich were doing their best to reacquaint Sam with his stomach-churning anxiety.

"Talk to him, Sam. Once he's done with that monstrosity, he's gonna hotfoot it out of here to his last class and then to the airport. He's got a six o'clock flight out of Kennedy, and according to Ziggy, he makes it."

"You and my mother looked great dancing together the other night." The words took a clumsy trip over Sam's tongue.

Gooshie rubbed his chin, his eyes continuing to scan the page. "She's a great dancer, your mother."

"Didn't look like you were doing too badly yourself."

"I was just having some fun."

Sam cleared his throat. "You know, she's really glad

she's got you as a partner. It's not easy to keep up with her . . . when she dances.''

''Did she really say that?''

''What?''

''That she's glad I'm her partner.''

Gooshie met his eyes and Sam knew the words had clicked. Like slide-show photos, sadness, frustration, longing flitted inside the programmer's baby blues before he squelched them and delved back into his book.

''Oh yeah. It means everything to her that you agreed to audition. She's really come to depend on you.''

''It's Marty she depends on. Not me.''

''You are her Marty.''

''No . . .'' He breathed out a cynical laugh. ''Believe me. I'm not.''

''I don't think I understand.''

Gooshie took another swig of milk and gazed off into the distance. ''Cary Grant once said something like his greatest aspiration was to be . . . Cary Grant. He was suave, charming, sensitive. Marty became all those things too, after your mother changed him from a frog into a prince.''

''But . . .''

''I was never an outgoing person, always kept to myself, nose in a book, typical brainy nerd. I took dancing lessons when I was a teenager. Thought it would help me get dates. It didn't but at least I found something I was good at besides calculus.'' He ripped off a chunk of bread and chewed it thoughtfully. ''I'd put that talent behind me for a long time. But one night last June, a few weeks after I started at NYU, it was so hot I just had to get out. Went to the Starlight on a whim, met Gerda. I swear, we danced until they threw us out.''

Al hunkered down, looking up into to Gooshie's face. ''Keep going, Sam. I think you're getting to him.''

"You know, I can tell a lot about people when they dance," Sam said.

Gooshie let out a ragged breath, then pressed his lips together, his eyes clamoring for the safety of his book again.

"You and my mom, it's like . . . you were meant to be together."

"No." He shook his head and smiled a sad little smile. "We have fun together, a few laughs, a little song and dance . . ."

That sadness praying on him would carry over well into the future. The Gooshie at Project Quantum Leap would continue to hide himself, not behind a book, but behind the paragon of advanced artificial intelligence Sam Beckett would create. Sam gave him Ziggy, but could he make him accept Gerda into his life before the computer even came to be? And if he did, would Gooshie feel compelled to pursue his career to the point where he would cross paths with Dr. Sam Beckett, quantum physicist, and impress the hell out of him? It was a crapshoot, a chance he had to take. He put the silent question to Al, who replied by nodding at him to go on.

"I don't know what your long-range goals are, Mr. Gushman." Sam's licked his lips, which had gone as dry as his throat. "Judging by that physics textbook you're reading, you're an educated man."

Gooshie shrugged and fingered the edge of a page, still not meeting Sam's gaze.

"A man with your intelligence can just about pick and choose his livelihood. Why would you want to spoil such a bright future by having to wonder what might have been?"

Giving up, Gooshie slapped the book closed. He seemed

dazed and morose as he rewrapped the remnants of his sandwich.

"I know I'm kind of overstepping my bounds here," Sam said slowly. "If you get up and leave, I'll completely understand."

"No-o. Don't give him any ideas!" Al winced and began to pace the length of the bench.

"But what good is success if you don't have someone special to share it with?"

Gooshie shoved the sandwich into the rumpled paper bag. "I like being by myself."

"You may think so now—"

"You talk much older than your years." Gooshie looked at him hard. Sam could almost believe he could peer through the aura to see the man who would someday play a vital part in his life.

"My age has nothing to do with what I've gone through. And I have a feeling you've lived through more than your share of tough times. Lonely times."

Gooshie dipped his head. His book, his safety hatch, was now closed on his lap; he had nowhere to hide. "Your mother and I . . . are years apart."

"Are you really though? When you care for someone, age is just a number."

He seemed to consider Sam's words, raising his head slowly, gazing at the activity at the other end of the park. "No," he said, finally. "No, I'm better off alone."

"Yeah, well . . ." Sam let out a short breath. "I guess it's easier that way. You'll never have to face the hurt of losing her. But is the trade-off worth it?"

"What . . . trade-off?"

"The trade-off of never knowing the rest of the story."

They stared at each other for a long moment. Gooshie opened his mouth to speak, but then closed it and shook his head slowly. He got up, tossed the sandwich bag into a wrought-iron trash barrel and rasped, "I've got to get to class." Hitching his book and folder under his arm, he hunched his shoulders, ducked his head and escaped down the path leading out of the park.

Sam remained seated, the aroma of Gooshie's lunch hovering over him like a ghost. "I think I just signed Gerda's death warrant."

Al twirled his cigar in his mouth, checking the link. "Ziggy says as of now, Gerda still dies, but she also says it's too soon to tell if your little pep talk might have changed that. We'll just have to wait and see."

Sam got up, shoved his hands in his pockets and kicked at some pebbles. "I don't understand it, Al. Nothing's working out on this Leap. It's like every step forward brings me two steps back."

Al squinted down the path Gooshie had taken. "It sure as hell seems that way, doesn't it?"

"I don't know what else to do."

"You're only human, Sam. You can't always succeed."

Sam jerked a thumb at the sky. "He seems to think I should."

Removing his cigar from his lips, Al blew out a stream of smoke and rocked back on his heels. "I guess that's because your track record is so damn good."

Sam ran his shoe along the edge of the grass. "Would you do me a favor?"

"Sure."

"Check on Rebecca for me."

"She's with Gerda, yakking it up."

"I know." One corner of Sam's mouth quirked. "But would you do it anyway?"

"Yeah, sure, Sam. I'll be right back. Just . . . hang in there." He gave Sam a wary frown before popping out.

The day was cool but Sam could feel a trickle of sweat making its way down his spine. He ran his hand along the top of the bench, staring at the stones, mossy patches and bits of glass at his feet, the knot in his stomach tightening with each step he took.

"Al?" he whispered. "Something's wrong, Al. I know it. I feel it."

The imaging chamber door slid open behind him, but Sam remained focused on the ground.

"Sam." The voice behind him was tight with urgency. "We've got a problem."

CHAPTER THIRTY-ONE

Only now could Gerda tell how warm the house was. Before, sitting with Rebecca at the piano, practicing a simple vocalise, she'd been unaware of the stuffiness of the room. Now, kneeling by Rebecca's locked bedroom door, her ear pressed to the wood, she realized how uncomfortable she had been for the past couple of hours. The house needed a good airing. Those heavy drapes in the living room blocked the sunlight and cut off the flow of air, (if the windows were open at all) making the place as close as a tomb.

''Rebecca.'' Gerda rapped softly on the door. ''Rebecca, honey. Please let me in so we can talk.'' She didn't know why she should even be thinking of her own discomfort now, in light of what had happened. In a matter of moments, her elation had turned to dread. Gerda was still dazed, trying to pile the events on top of one another like building blocks. Had she done or said something to cause Rebecca to dissolve into such a frenzied state? Gerda had seen women snap before. In 1950, at the height of Wildwood's summer season, Lainie Austwerp went nuts and threw a steak knife at the entertainment director, when he told her to change a few steps in her dance routine.

Rebecca hadn't turned violent like Lainie, or if she had, it was only to hurt herself. The thought made Gerda's eyes sting with hot tears. She pressed her ear harder against the door, attempting to hear a breath, a sob, a cough—any sign of life.

"Rebecca?"

Earlier, a young lady with auburn curls, clad in jeans and an Elton John T-shirt, had knocked and entered while Rebecca was running through Gerda's fifth vocal exercise: *Me Mi My Mo Mu.* Gerda recalled how she'd mirrored Rebecca's example, forming her lips into a perfect *O* as she sang those syllables. The simple exercise enabled her to round her tones, and she was amazed at the wonderful new clarity of sound emanating from her own mouth. While she was vocalizing, Gerda noticed how the girl's knees quivered, how her eyes shimmered with excitement, as she waited for Rebecca to acknowledge her. She was bursting with some kind of fantastic news, and Gerda found herself on tenterhooks to hear it.

After playing the final chord, Rebecca turned her attention to the girl. "Betsy, thank you for being so patient. It's good to see you, but I didn't think our lesson was until tomorrow."

"I know, but I just had to tell you today."

"You heard? So soon?"

Betsy knelt and took Rebecca's hands. "I got the part,"

she whispered, her smile growing broader until it reached from ear to ear. "I'm Shana."

"Omigod, omigod, omigod!" Rebecca stood and hugged Betsy so hard, Gerda worried that girl's bones might snap. The two remained that way, their sniffles and giggles erupting into tiny shrieks of triumph. Finally, they released each other, wiping their eyes with the palms of their hands, letting out the residual peals of laughter.

Rebecca patted Gerda's shoulder. "Gerda, this is Betsy Damon, one of my prize pupils who's just gotten her first costarring role on Broadway."

Gerda got off the bench, clapped her hands and let out a joyous whoop. "That is wonderful, sweetheart." She pumped the girl's hand with unrestrained enthusiasm. "Good luck to you."

"Thanks. I'm sorry to have interrupted your lesson. It's just that I never would have gotten the nerve to go for the audition if it wasn't for Rebecca." She held her hand to her chest, breathless. "I never would have considered myself good enough, but when she told me she thought I had a shot, I just had to try." She turned to Rebecca again. "That's why I had to come tell you in person and invite you to my celebration dinner tonight at Tavern on the Green."

The first block fell into place. That's when the trouble started. At that moment Rebecca's smile failed her; it was then she took an unsteady step back and ran two fingers through her hair. "Oh . . . I'm sorry . . . I can't make it . . ."

"Oh." Betsy's smile faded, but she brightened after a moment. "Our first rehearsal is a week from tomorrow. It would mean so much to me if you could be there."

The second block tumbled on top of the first. Rebecca took another step back and leaned against the piano for support. She blinked at the lamp, then gazed at the sheet music as if it all belonged to someone else. "I would," she murmured, "but it's not safe."

The statement was made with such detached calm, Gerda was not sure if she had heard correctly. It was only when Rebecca stumbled forward and hissed those words over and over that Gerda realized her ears were not playing tricks on her. Rebecca's eyes widened; she clasped her chest and sobbed. *Not safe anymore, not safe, not safe.* She drew in breaths with a strangled keening sound, then ran to the bedroom, slamming the door behind her.

Betsy sobbed, her face holding a look of revulsion and fear. "What did I say? Did I do something wrong?"

"Of course not, dear," Gerda escorted her to the door. "Sometimes people get so excited, it affects them the wrong way." She winked, inwardly taken aback by her own sense of calm. "Rebecca just needs to rest up a bit and she'll be fine."

"What about my lesson tomorrow?"

Gerda stole a look at the closed bedroom door, then willed herself to smile at Betsy. "We'll call you. Don't worry, okay?"

"Okay. Tell her I hope she feels better."

"I will." Gerda watched the girl walk slowly down the porch steps, then she shifted her gaze to the wind chimes tinkling in the afternoon breeze. She stood rooted to the spot, her thoughts spiraling off into eighty directions. Should she call a doctor? No, what if this type of episode was commonplace and Rebecca had just gone to take her medicine? But what if that wasn't the case? What if she was laid out on the bed, unconscious. She raced to the bedroom door and knocked. "Rebecca . . . ?" The knob was stiff and unyielding in her hand. Jiggling it hard, she shouted, "Rebecca?"

But Rebecca was too busy to respond. She was singing

the same refrain over and over, her voice high and sweet, the melody light and lilting. It might have been a childrens' song—something about being in her own little corner in her own little chair.

Gerda clenched her fingers over the thick pile of the carpet, then pushed herself up. She moved to the desk in the music room, found the student roster and began canceling lessons for the rest of the week . . .

Now the weariness crept over her like a warm sea. Recalling her ordeal was almost as exhausting as going through it, and it reminded her that she was no spring chicken anymore. No use mulling over that now. Checking her watch, she exhaled softly. It had been quiet in the room for almost an hour. Gerda's knees were sore from kneeling so long. She turned back to the bedroom, eased down on her behind with her legs crossed Indian style and knocked again, hoping for a response that didn't come. In another five or ten minutes she would have to call the police. The thought of uncaring strangers barging in here wearing their big shoes, guns and uniforms unnerved her. They would hammer her and Rebecca with questions. And what if the press got wind of it? Wouldn't that ruin Rebecca's career? No, Gerda decided, she would wait for Noah. Besides, wasn't that a sigh and the rustle of bedding she'd just heard through the door? Rebecca was asleep. That's all.

Did she have family? A close friend to call in an emergency? Everyone had someone, didn't they? Marty came to mind. Who did *he* have . . . besides her? Gerda didn't know. There were so many things she didn't know about him . . .

When Noah returned, they would decide together what to do about Rebecca. The thought of her son made her scowl. Which one of his schleppy friends, she wondered, was in trouble dire enough to warrant Noah leaving work for him? Such a nerve! Noah's place was *here*, helping her with this problem instead of leaving her alone. But of course she was being irrational and unfair. Noah wasn't a fortune-teller, a mind reader. He couldn't see the future. How was he supposed to know all hell was going to break loose when he left? Gerda held her head in her hands and took three deep breaths to compose herself.

She refused to allow herself to sink into melancholia. As a performer, she'd put on her best face every time she went onstage, even when she knew Danny was giving a different type of performance between the perfumed sheets of Rosalie, or Lila, or Marcie. Now she'd have to dredge up some of that old showbiz gusto to help this girl before she sank deeper into whatever kind of dark hole she had dug for herself. The plan hatching in her head was pure hokum, she thought, as she used the doorknob to pull herself up. But it might work. Yes, it *could* work to charm Rebecca into opening the door. She smoothed her jacket, cleared her throat, then rounded her lips and ran through her vocalise twice. "How was that?" she asked the door. No response. "Tough crowd. Guess you're waiting for the big stuff, huh? Well, you want it, honey? You got it." And with that, she burst into a version of "Lullaby" brash enough to set the floorboards jumping.

CHAPTER THIRTY-TWO

So it had come to this.

Rebecca's shivering had abated, but still she held the two quilts and the sheet up to her chin, and gazed around the room where she was to spend the rest of her life. In a way, it was a comfort to know how safe she was going to feel from now on.

You can't.

Betsy's news had driven her to the only safe zone left. Now she knew she would never step out her front door again, not because she didn't want to—it all came down to self-preservation. Her throat would close up if she went outside; her heart would shrink to that chip of granite from her nightmare, and she would die. The thought made the tips of her fingers tingle and her stomach churn. She swallowed hard and slunk deeper into her bedding, where it was safe.

Her compunction to meet with students in the music room would soon leave her. They deserved better anyway. Poor Betsy. She closed her eyes and pictured the girl's pretty features twisting in horror. Betsy would survive the incident; she'd get involved in rehearsals. Her mother would hire a new voice teacher and everyone would go on with their lives.

You can't you can't you can't

Someone was singing just outside her door. She hitched herself up on her elbows to listen. It was Gerda. A half smile lifted a corner of her mouth. Why was she still here? How long had she been at it? Rebecca had been concentrating so hard on making herself feel better, she'd heard nothing but the sound of her own mantras for the past hour. Gerda held one tremulous note for what seemed like a minute and a half. Rebecca wanted to tell her to bring it up from her middle, not from her throat. She would strain her vocal cords doing that.

Nero fiddled while Rome burned. The *Titanic* sank, and the band played on. Rebecca Wexler was fading fast, while Gerda Ellman's voice rang out to cheer her.

The song came to its bombastic finish, and Gerda immediately started on another one. "Melancholy Baby." Perfect . . .

Gerda meant well, but soon she would give up. Noah would too, now that he knew what he'd gotten himself into. They would leave her and go on with their lives. Outside . . .

youcantyoucantyoucantyoucant

She buried her head in her pillow and rocked from side to side, willing away that persistent voice in her head, wishing Gerda's singing were powerful enough to drown it out.

CHAPTER THIRTY-THREE

It was the longest train ride of Sam's life. At Times Square he had boarded the A train back to Brooklyn. Unfortunately, he discovered too late, it was a local. As they rolled to a stop every two minutes, he followed their snail-like progress on the subway map posted near the middle door of the car. By the time they'd reached the tenth stop, he had the compulsion to hurl himself out of the train and run the rest of the way back to Rebecca's. Groaning with frustration, he pressed his forehead against the grimy window as an express train roared past them down the center track.

"You should have waited another five minutes, Sam." Al squinted at the map along with him. "You could have been on that one."

"Yeah, well, no one had the foresight to tell me that."

The link squawked.

"Would you please go stay with Rebecca, Al?"

"She's layin' in her bed, mumbling to herself, while Gerda's serenading her outside the door. What good can I do her? I'm a hologram." He passed through the window two times to prove his point. "And I think at this stage of the game, you need me more."

Sam placed a palm against the glass, gritting his teeth as the train huffed to a stop again. "Please . . ." Knowing Al was in a place he needed to be gave Sam a great emotional lift. No, Al couldn't ease Rebecca's pain, but at least he could be a positive force hovering over her. And sometimes, in some inexplicable way, his unnoticed presence did a lot of good.

"Okay, okay, I'm gone." Al tapped two buttons on the link and winked out.

When the train finally reached the Flatbush Avenue station, Sam propelled himself through the door and up the stairs, as if he had jet packs on his feet. Rebecca's house was two blocks away, and he took them like a marathon sprinter. He burst through the door just as Gerda was finishing up the last chorus of "Melancholy Baby."

"Noah." Gerda gripped his hand. "Rebecca locked herself in her room after one of her students asked her to come to a rehearsal. One minute she was fine, the next she just—"

"She's agoraphobic, Mom." Sam pressed his ear to the door.

"What does *that* mean?"

"It's a panic disorder. She can't go anywhere she doesn't feel 'safe,' which right now seems to be anywhere but her room—"

Al poked his head through the wood, startling Sam, sending him rearing back.

"What's wrong?" Gerda's hand tightened around his.

"Nothing, just a crick in my neck, that's all." He rolled his head against his shoulders for effect.

"Rebecca's okay, Sam. She's just lying there, staring at the ceiling."

"If you knew she was sick, Noah, why didn't you get her to a doctor instead of gallivanting off like that?" Gerda scowled. "If anyone needed your help today, it was her."

"It's not the kind of sick you can fix with chicken soup and aspirin, Mom."

Suddenly the knob rattled, clicked and twisted. "Come in," said the small tremulous voice just beyond the door.

"I've never told this to anybody."

She lay on the bed beneath the quilts, her blond hair lank around her face. Sam sat by her side, Gerda in a chair in the corner. Al paced by the half-open door, cigar smoke draping him like a veil.

"It was a secret I managed to keep for almost two years."

"Why didn't you go for help?" Sam asked softly.

She swallowed and fingered the ends of her hair. "I needed to prove I could take care of myself without David around."

"David?"

"He was my fiancé. We met at UCLA, where we were both getting our master's degrees in music. We were so right for each other. Soul mates, he called us." She breathed out a ragged laugh. "Sounds like something out of a bad romance novel. But it was the only way to describe what we had."

"After we graduated, he returned with me to New York, against his parents' wishes. They gave him a real hard time, mostly because they didn't think I was good enough for him. They were very wealthy; his father was in the oil business. David was their only child.'' She raised her eyes to the ceiling. ''And I don't think any woman, except maybe Jackie Kennedy Onassis, would have met with their approval.

''Our first year together was just . . . golden. He found work on Madison Avenue, writing commercial jingles. I set up a few classes here, while applying for teaching jobs. He barely spoke to his parents . . .''

''What about your family?'' Sam asked.

''My mother and I have been estranged ever since she remarried five years ago. Her new husband controls her. He wanted to control me too, until I told him where to get off.'' Her lips tightened. ''She knows where I am, if she wants to see me.''

''Your dad?''

''Dad and my brother are archaeologists. They live in London, but spend most of their time on digs in the Middle East. We exchange Christmas cards, with cheery little ramblings about how the year went . . .''

''You've been alone, really alone, for a long time.'' Her hand was cold beneath his.

''David was my anchor. When he . . . died, it was like I was set adrift. I haven't returned yet. I don't think I ever will. I guess I never thought I'd lose him. We never think anyone we love can be yanked out of our lives that suddenly.'' She closed her eyes, took a few deep breaths, recouping her strength, then looked at Sam again. ''It was a Tuesday. He left for work wearing jeans instead of dress pants, because his boss was on vacation and everyone was taking advantage of it in little ways. He kissed me at the door and asked me if I wanted to see a movie that night. I told him we could decide later. That was the last time I saw him alive.'' Her lower lip trembled. ''Two guys waiting for the train down the platform from David were having an argument over a leather jacket. One of them pulled a gun, the other guy tried to get it away from him. It went off. The bullet deflected off a pole and hit David in the chest. I was told by some sadistic newspaper reporter that the whole incident took ninety seconds from start to finish.''

She closed her eyes and was silent for a while. The link chittered, soft as a cat's purr.

Taking a deep breath, she blinked some tears away and continued. ''David's parents came to New York to bring the body back to California. I remember thinking at the time that at least now they'd be civil to me. We would at least be able to mourn together.'' She shook her head as if to shake off the memory. ''But it didn't happen that way. They were more hostile to me than when David was alive. When I met them at their hotel, they told me it was my fault he was dead. If I hadn't 'lured' him away to New York, this never would have happened. The pain I felt couldn't have been worse if they had plunged a knife into my chest and twisted it.'' Her voice grew low. ''I think I muttered that I wished it had been me lying dead on that subway platform.''

Sam clasped her hand tighter. ''Did they comfort you then?''

Rebecca's eyes glittered cold as she met his gaze. ''No. They agreed with me.''

''Migod,'' Al muttered.

Gerda hitched back a sob.

''The rest of that week is pretty much a blur. I was out of it most of the time, walking around in a fog. The only clear memory I have is of standing by the window in the airport, watching the plane carrying David's body leave the runway, growing more distant until it was just a dot against the blue sky . . ." She lifted her free hand as if to catch it. "Until it was gone."

Her other hand was warmer now. She blinked at the ceiling and sighed. "After that, I decided to stay at home for a while. The outside world held nothing for me anymore. It's amazing how easily you can survive with a roof over your head, a credit card and a telephone."

"You stopped applying for teaching jobs outside?"

"I actually turned down two. Nothing mattered anymore."

"Your kids mattered," Sam said gently.

"Yes," she agreed. "They literally saved my life. If I hadn't had their lessons to plan and their talents to hone, I doubt I would have kept myself going. Especially when I discovered I wasn't able to walk out my front door."

"You didn't know . . . ?"

"I think subconciously I was aware of it. But it wasn't until five weeks later, when I decided to go out for a newspaper and couldn't manage to step onto the front porch, that the reality of my situation set in."

"Did you know you had a treatable disease?" Sam tried to keep his voice even.

"I did. But it was my secret. My problem. I felt I could deal with it on my own, and eventually it would go away."

"But that wasn't the case."

"No. It's gotten worse. I have nightmares from it, where I can't get to my safe spot. I gouged my nails into my palms in my sleep"—she held up her bandaged hands—"from sheer terror. I guess I . . . lied about the cactus." The corner of her mouth quirked. "And today . . ." A tear slipped down her cheek. "Well, you know what happened today—" Her sobs came in long, breathy gasps. Sam leaned forward, giving her shoulders a tentative caress. He was fearful of taking her in his arms, not wanting a replay of last night's emotional tilt-a-whirl. But it was she who embraced him this time, making him catch his breath. Her slim frame trembled against his chest, her weeping intensified as she clasped him to her tighter. Another anchor, he thought, tightening his embrace. But he couldn't allow her to depend on him either. It was only a matter of time before he Leaped. Then the real Noah would return. While he might be sympathetic, he wouldn't be much of an anchor. His memory would be so fuzzy he might not even remember her.

"Sam, Ziggy says she never gets the help she needs. She's still a recluse in our time." Al's rendering of the data put a capper on Sam's doomy meanderings.

"You're not alone anymore."

Sam turned his head to see Gerda approach. Her steps were quick and confident as she dabbed her eyes with a tissue. She seated herself on the opposite side of the bed and stroked Rebecca's hair.

"Thank you for those songs, Gerda." Rebecca took Gerda's hand and pressed it to her cheek. "I know you couldn't tell from out there, but they really helped."

"That's what I'm here for—to help. You've had a rough time of it."

She nodded into Sam's shirt.

"I can sympathize with what you've gone through. I know all about disappointment and regret. They feed on you. They'll kill you if you let them, honey. You have to get out there and enjoy your life again, not give up on it. And I'm going to help you do that."

"Sam. Everything's changing." Al eyes widened at the link. "You're not going to believe this."

"Come here, honey." Gerda reached for Rebecca, who

released herself from Sam to fall into the woman's embrace.

"Gerda becomes Rebecca's primary caregiver, helping her to find a therapist and accompanying her to appointments." He cocked his head, his smile wistful. "Even though Gooshie leaves her in the lurch, she's okay because she devotes the next couple of years to making sure Rebecca gets well. She's got a purpose, Sam."

She doesn't die? Sam mouthed.

"Oh, well, yeah, in about ten years." Al hitched one shoulder. "But that's ten years longer than she would have lived otherwise."

Sam was glad to see Rebecca smile, glad for Gerda's renewed purpose in life. But he couldn't help feeling cheated. He wanted Gooshie to be at that ballroom tomorrow night. Gooshie owed Gerda that dance, even if it was the last one they would ever have.

CHAPTER THIRTY-FOUR

"Why don't you do yourself a favor and get some rest?" Sam sat outside Hop Joy's, waiting for the food he'd ordered for Gerda, Rebecca and himself. This time he'd made a list of their requests, and didn't diverge from it by even one wonton. Al paced before him, puffing his cigar. His face bore a hint of stubble, his eyes were red-rimmed, weary.

"I should, huh? It's been one hell of a long day. But I didn't want to leave until everything had calmed down."

Sam hung one arm over the back of the bench, giving his head an inquisitive tilt. "Is Ziggy sure that Gooshie's not going to show?"

Al raised an eyebrow at the link. "The percentages are

hovering around the eighty-seven percent mark. He's already checked out of that fleabag hotel he was holed up in."

"Mad Mountain Dina must be devastated."

"Yeah." Al chuckled. "She must be stomping those big feet to beat the band."

"Did he make his flight?"

"No. Now . . . this is strange. He was supposed to take flight one seventy-six out of Kennedy tonight, but that's changed. Now he's leaving tomorrow at three P.M."

Sam tapped his lower lip with a forefinger. "Second thoughts?"

"Don't get your hopes up, Sam." Al tapped his cigar, its ashes vanishing to the oblivion of the chamber floor. "He probably just wanted to get a good night's sleep before making the cross-country trip."

"So . . . why haven't I Leaped?"

"I guess you still have a few more things to put right." Al yawned, then gave a perfunctory glance at the screen. "Ziggy says you'll figure it out."

"What does that mean?"

"Exactly what it says. Ziggy also says good night, by the way."

"Night, Ziggy." Sam wiggled his fingers at the link.

"She also says support your local union." Al grimaced as he stepped through the chamber door and into its glow. "I'll see you tomorrow—at the Starlight."

The door whooshed shut. Sam clicked his tongue and shoved his hands into his pockets. He swallowed hard and attempted to shrug off the envy and frustration that hit him each time Al returned to the complex—which was now not much more than a washed-out watercolor in Sam's muddled memory. *A few more things to put right.* He forced his thoughts back to the here and now. Yes, he had to be at the ballroom to comfort Gerda when Gooshie didn't show. There was no way around that. If Sam Leaped out now, the real Noah would still be too blitzed from his Leap experience to be any help to her at all. But he couldn't help wondering if there was another reason too. From behind, a knock on the window jarred him. He swiveled his head to see the woman displaying two brown paper bags, one in each hand, and motioning at him with her head. Pushing himself off the bench, he headed for the door. He placed a hand on the push bar, but then paused, turning to gaze up at the star-dappled sky. A slow smile spread across his face, as he wondered why this idea had been so long in coming. It would be the icing on the cake, if he could pull it off. *Yes*, he thought, entering the restaurant. *Yes.*

Arms filled with packages, Sam ambled up the path to Rebecca's. The porch light clicked on, and Gerda stepped out, setting the wind chimes tinkling. She threw him a puzzled frown. "What the hell is all this stuff, Noah? Did you bring home a banquet?"

"No," he grunted, handing the Hop Joy bags to her, while hefting the larger packages higher in his arms. "The bigger bags are for Rebecca."

"A surprise?"

"Yeah."

"What's in them?"

"You'll see." He smiled as he moved past her, but she caught his arm before he could make it to the stairs.

"I got her to come back into the music room and sit on the sofa," she whispered. "It wasn't easy. She started to shake so bad, I thought I was going to have to let her go back to bed. But we both persevered." She moved her hand down to lightly touch his fingers. "I don't want to leave her alone if I don't have to. After dinner I'll go home for some clothes and sleep here tonight. Tomorrow we're going to let our fingers do the walking and shop for doctors. What's the matter, Noah? You've got that funny look in your eyes again, like you did when you first saw Marty."

He cleared his throat and shrugged. "It's just amazing how things work out sometimes."

"Yeah, ain't it?" Gerda did a neat two-step, her short heels clacking against the sidewalk. "Let's eat."

CHAPTER THIRTY-FIVE

Sam didn't realize how hungry he was until the cardboard containers were opened and the smells of spareribs, pork fried rice, soup, eggrolls and lo mein, filled the kitchen. Rebecca sat at the head of the butcher block table, watching him and Gerda set the plastic utensils and napkins in place, her eyes shining bright with excitement.

"I can't remember the last time anyone took care of me."

Sam poured her a glass of iced tea, while Gerda spooned rice onto her plate. "Everyone needs to be pampered now and then," Gerda said. "You've got to learn to take as well as give." She paused, the spoon halfway between the plate and the cardboard container. "That sounds strange coming from me, huh, Noah?"

"Guess you're going to have to learn to take some of your own advice." He took the spoon from her and placed it on a napkin. Then he took her arm and led her to the chair next to Rebecca. "Sit."

"But I'm not done—"

"Sit." Pulling the chair out, he patted the seat cushion. "My name is Noah," he said, bowing low, "and I will be your waiter this evening. Your wish"—he threw a kiss at the air and wink at Rebecca, who giggled with delight—"is my command."

"My son the charmer," Gerda gushed.

Sam sat across from Rebecca and clinked his glass with his fork. "Before we dig in to this delectable array of edibles, I wish to propopse a toast."

"A toast!" The women set their utensils down and raised their glasses.

"To better days."

"To better days," they echoed, and then they all clinked each other's glass one by one.

Amen to that, thought Sam, swigging his tea.

As promised, Sam had played waiter and busboy to the hilt, clearing the table and washing the dishes, while Gerda went back to her apartment to pack an overnight bag. Now Rebecca sat on the sofa next to Sam, more at ease and happy than she had been since he'd met her. Her features were relaxed, if weary. Her legs were curled beneath her, her hair pulled back into a ponytail. She looked like a schoolgirl home from a long, difficult semester.

"I feel I need to apologize for what happened on the porch yesterday—and for afterward when I was so rude to you. But I was frightened. You saw what was beneath the mask—the real Rebecca," she said.

Inwardly, he shuddered at the comment, which cut much too close. "You don't have to apologize, Rebecca." He leaned his head to one side and smiled, stroking her cheek with the back of his hand. *So pretty,* he thought. Neither her pallor nor the shadows beneath her eyes took away from her glow, the inner beauty that could not be squelched.

"I should have been honest with you from the start. I should have told you about my agoraphobia and the 'safe zones' I have to adhere to."

"Fear makes its own decisions for you sometimes. But that part is over now. Once you admit you need help, you've got half the battle won." He smiled.

She fingered the edge of the thick curtain, averting her eyes from his. "You remind me of David so much—your gentleness, your compassion, even the way that one stubborn strand of hair keeps falling over your brow. That's what set me off."

He didn't like the way her lower lip was beginning to tremble. "Hey, I have a surprise for you."

She raised her head and peered over his shoulder. "I was wondering about those packages . . ."

"Yep." He strode to the door, lifted the bags and carried them to the couch, then set them on the floor. "Open this one first," he said, indicating the smaller of the two.

She tossed him a bewildered glance, then leaned over to slide the bag closer. "What is this?"

"Open it."

"I don't know if I like surprises."

"You'll like this one."

With a light shrug, she unfolded the top of the bag, then peered inside. She wrinkled her nose, then raised her head again. "It's dirt."

''Yep.''

''It's a big plastic bag filled with dirt.''

''Yep.'' Sam nodded, crossing his arms.

''Did you think my dream in life was to make mud pies in the center of my music room?'' Her eyes glimmered with amusement.

''Well, some of your younger students might enjoy that.''

They dissolved into giggles as Rebecca continued to squint into the bag. ''Dirt!'' She raised a forefinger in realization. ''I know. You're really a traveling salesman, who's finally got the lady of the house where he wants her. There's a new handy dandy vacuum in that other bag. You're going to prove to me how wonderful it works by pouring out the dirt and sucking it all up in less than three minutes.''

''Wrong!'' Sam dragged the other bag closer to the sofa. ''But a terrific guess. Johnny, tell her what she's won.''

Rebecca took the bag from him, but she was shaking so hard with laughter that she couldn't manage to open it.

''Need some help?'' His mock serious tone caused her laughter to reach new stratospheres. It was a few minutes before she was able to scrub the tears from the corners of her eyes and regain her composure.

''Now,'' she said, letting out a residual giggle. ''Where were we?''

''Your consolation prize, ma'am.''

She opened the bag and pulled out a long green sprig. ''It's an evergreen.''

Sam twiddled an imaginary cigar à la Groucho. ''You just said the magic woid. And there's lots more where that came from.''

''You're right,'' she said, rooting through the bag. ''Okay, I'll bite. What's all this about?''

''It's for your window boxes.'' He dug a transparent plastic box from his trouser pocket and handed it to her.

Her smile faded slightly as she ran one finger over it. ''Why are you giving me a dead butterfly, Noah?''

''I thought you might want to keep him. He was your boarder. The window box was his final home.''

She covered the box with her hands, as if to warm it. ''Thank you.''

''I knew how much you like plants, and that at one time your window boxes must have contained something other than a dead insect.''

''That's true,'' Rebecca said quietly. ''I used to plant geraniums, but that was a while ago.''

''I wanted you to be able to put something in there when you felt better, something that didn't require a whole lot of care. Besides, it'll be winter soon . . .''

''Evergreen sprigs in the dirt.'' She fingered the edge of the bag and gazed at Sam in amazement.

''The lady in the flower shop suggested it as something that would look nice and not die on you in the cold weather.'' He took her hand. ''What do you think?''

She leaned close, so close he could see gold flecks in the blue of her irises. Then she showed him what she thought—kissing him once, twice, and again, her gentleness belying a suppressed passion both of them knew it would not be wise to kindle.

''Thank you, Noah.'' She kissed him once more, then shifted back an inch, her hands flitting over his shoulders, his hands, before settling back into her lap.

''For what?''

She sighed, her lips sporting a wisp of a grin. ''For not walking away.''

CHAPTER THIRTY-SIX

It was a special night. The room beyond the lobby glittered with starlight, buoyed by a musical cloud. He glanced down at her, the lady that spangled and sparkled in black, waiting to get out there and strut her stuff. Given the chance, she would floor those judges. Her face was so full of hope and purpose, and Sam wished he could somehow divert the disappointment he knew was forthcoming. The events of the past two days played in his head. He thought of Rebecca's renewed confidence and her determination to get well. Earlier, he and Gerda had gone to Brooklyn Hospital and met with a doctor who agreed to take Rebecca's case. They were referred to Dr. Amarante, a staff therapist, by one of the nurses. He did a lot of work with panic disorder victims, she'd told them, and his success rate was high. Hearing how severe Rebecca's agoraphobia was, he had agreed to conduct the first few sessions with her at the house, starting next week. Something positive had come out of this Leap, Sam told himself. At least Rebecca was in good hands. And as far as Gooshie went, well, no one could say Sam hadn't tried.

Al swaggered out of the glowing portal, his cigar planted firmly between two fingers. He was dressed to kill in a sparkling black tux and cummerbund, looking like a mogul straight out of Hollywood's golden age.

"Noah, I'm going to freshen up, then I'll go sign in. Wait out here for Marty." Gerda made her way through the milling throng. Just inside the entranceway she was stopped by Mary Jane Wax and Jason. The sequins on Mary Jane's dress sparkled as brightly as the gleam in her eyes. She hugged Gerda, then kissed her cheek and wished her luck. Gerda threw a knowing look first at her, then Jason. Then, chuckling like a mischievous child, she moved into the ballroom, shaking hands and waving at those who called her name.

Sam edged himself into a corner, and set his gaze out the plate glass window overlooking the parking lot. "You look like Metro-Goldwyn-Mayer all rolled into one," he muttered through the side of his mouth.

"Yeah, well last time here, I wasn't able to enjoy myself too much." Al sneered at the handlink.

"And you're thinking of having a party tonight? Gooshie's not gonna show. His flight left hours ago. In a half hour I'll be drying Gerda's tears off my suit."

"Now, Sam." Al hitched a brow at him. "I've never known you to be a pessimist."

"You can't blame me this time—Al?" Sam narrowed his eyes at his friend. "What's going on, Al?"

Al twirled the cigar between his teeth, giving Sam a sidelong glance. "Gooshie wasn't on that plane."

"No . . . ?"

"He switched his flight again, to flight eight seventeen, which takes off tomorrow at four in the afternoon. Then he rented a car . . ."

"So you think he's had second thoughts?"

Al gave him a look. "Don't you?"

"I don't know, Al." Sam pressed his palm against the glass and scanned the lot. "He's had plenty of time to get here. Why would he be late?"

A fanfare blared from the ballroom, then an announcement was made over the loudspeaker. "Better go check on Gerda, Sam. I'll let you know if I see him."

Inside, the crowd had gathered around the bandstand. A familiar-looking man, his silver blond hair longish and swept back, stood at the microphone. Clad in a white sequined suit, he flashed a smile as bright as the mirror ball rotating above him. As he explained the rules of the audition, Sam remembered where he'd seen him before—as the host of the "You Can Be a Star" television show. His name was something singsongy, like Tweedledee and Tweedledum. Sam struggled to remember, while the host told a overly long anecdote about his beginnings in show biz. Gerard Jerome! That was it. He recalled the rapture on Gerda's face when she watched him at home. She was no less enthralled by him now, as she stood openmouthed at the side of the stage, awestruck as a smitten teen.

When Gerard's spiel was done, the orchestra swung into a jaunty rendition of "That's Entertainment." The crowd moved back, clearing the dance floor for the performers, as Gerda rushed over to Sam, grabbing his arm and pulling him over to the wall. "Where is Marty?"

"I . . . I didn't see him, Mom." *Here it comes.* He craned

his neck, moving his head from side to side to see over the crowd.

"We're supposed to be on first!" She tightened her grip on his arm, her eyes scanning as much of the room as she could see.

Sam jostled for position, as a juggling troupe pushed by him, heading toward the roped-off section set aside for the contestants. Gerard stood at the side of the bandstand, rifling through his papers. Sam looked at Gerda, who suddenly seemed so frightened, so lost. The thought of her falling apart on him in the middle of the ballroom caused a slow ache to rise from his stomach to his chest. He wanted to lead her out of here, to take her back to Rebecca's. She had found comfort there, purpose. In time she'd forget this disappointment. He took her by the arm but she pulled back.

"What are you doing?" she asked.

"Maybe we should . . . go back to Rebecca's."

"You're crazy, Noah." She wrenched away from him. "Go wait out there for Marty. I'm going to see if they'll let us go second."

With great reluctance, he turned and walked toward the lobby, glancing back only once to see her wringing her hands, waiting by the bandstand for Gerard to deign to acknowledge her. Sam entered the lobby, the sound of "That's Entertainment" diminishing as the door swung closed behind him.

"What the hell are you doing, Sam? Stay with Gerda." Al puffed his cigar and stood in the lobby, which had cleared out. "I'll let you know if he comes."

"She wants me to wait out here and keep an eye out for him, Al." He shook his head and plopped down on the sofa. "She still has hopes he'll show."

"Hmmph. It's getting kind of late."

"Yeah . . ."

Sam picked at an errant thread on his cuff and tapped his foot. Finally, his restlessness got the better of him. He pushed himself off the sofa and joined Al by the window. They stood side by side, gazing out, like two kids waiting for their lost dog to come home.

"What's that?" Sam pointed at a winking red glow wavering back and forth at the other end of the parking lot.

Al squinted at it. "Looks like someone pacing, smoking a cigarette. Want me to take a look?"

Sam's heart lurched. He bolted for the door, melting through the hologram in the process. "C'mon, Al."

"What makes you think it's him?" Al kept up with Sam, floating alongside him as he ran down a row of cars and turned right.

"Just a gut feeling, that's all." The red glow was stationary now, the figure leaning against a car. Sam slowed his step as he drew closer, heart lubdubbing, his chest heaving as he caught his breath.

"Son of a gun, Sam, I think you're right."

"Mr. Gushman," Sam called.

The red glow fell to the grass. The figure stamped on it, then fumbled with the door to his car, managing to pull it open just as Sam reached him.

"Mr. Gushman?" Sam peered into the driver's window, which was rolled up tight. Gooshie faced forward, twisting the key in the ignition. The engine caught, then rumbled, waiting for further instructions.

"Son of a gun," Al said.

Sam rapped on the glass. "Please, Mr. Gushman. Don't leave."

Gooshie's eyes flickered toward him for an instant, then back to the windshield.

"She's waiting for you . . . They're all . . . waiting."

Gooshie tapped the steering wheel with one finger, then pounded it with his palm. He grimaced and rolled down the window.

"Hi, Mr. Gushman."

"Hi, Noah."

Sam leaned his head into the car, forgetting Gooshie's demon halitosis in his haste. He was reminded quickly enough. Turning his head, he took a deep breath of fresh air, then coughed.

"Noah, have you ever seen your conscience?" Gooshie asked mildly.

"No." Sam choked and rubbed his watering eyes. "I can't say I have."

"Mine wears a brightly colored floral-designed shirt and smokes a cigar."

"Oh?" Sam gave his friend a look. Al responded by dipping his head and taking a sheepish step back.

"He talked to me the night before last. I was somewhat inebriated at the time, but still . . ."

"What did he say?"

"He said . . . if I didn't show up for the audition I was going to regret it."

"So . . . you're letting your conscience be your guide?" Sam asked.

"Then you just happened to meet me in the park the next day, and told me the same thing, basically." He ran his finger along the steering wheel, gazing out at the moon. "I'm not religious, Noah, but I do have a sense of spirituality. However, I did entertain thoughts of ignoring my gaudy conscience—"

"Hey, watch that." Al pouted.

"—and your very sensible argument and leaving for California today, where I'm going to be finishing up my studies."

"But you didn't."

"No, I postponed my flight . . . for the third time." Gooshie shook his head, leaning his hands on the dashboard. "At the airport, I was waiting in the lounge after checking my luggage, and the strangest thing happened—"

"Yeah?" Al's eyes grew big; Sam inched forward.

"There was some sort of problem with the muzak. It got so loud, people started running around, shouting, covering their ears."

"Yeah . . . ?" Sam said.

"When the song was over, the volume went back to normal." Gooshie snapped his fingers. "Just like that."

"I still don't understand," Sam told him.

Gooshie sighed and met his eyes. "The song was 'Lullaby Of Broadway,' and if I didn't know better, I would swear it was your mother singing. That's crazy, huh?"

"Crazy . . . ," Sam whispered.

"Geez, Louise," Al said.

They stared at each other in stunned silence.

"I switched my flight, drove around the city for a while before coming here. I'm still not sure if I'm going in." He looked up at the glowing marquee emblazoned with the legend GERARD JEROME IN PERSON! "YOU CAN BE A STAR"—AUDITIONS TONIGHT.

"You don't have much time to decide," Sam said, his voice tinged with desperation. He was so close, he couldn't back down now. "She already had to stall them once. I doubt if they'll let her do it again."

"Yeah." Gooshie narrowed his eyes at himself in the rearview, straightening the lapels of his tux. "I guess I don't have to be hit over the head again to see that I'm supposed to be here."

Sam pulled open the door. "You're going to make my mother very happy tonight, Gooshie."

He got out of the car slowly, giving Sam a strange look. "Gooshie?"

Oh boy. "Sorry, I meant, Mr. Gushman."

"No, it's quite all right. Gooshie. I . . . kind of like it." There was a spring in his step as he made his way through the parking lot toward the ballroom, his shiny black dress shoes clicking in buoyant time against the asphalt.

"He finally gave in." Al said, retrieving the blinking, chittering link from his tux jacket. "I never thought we'd see it happen."

"It's not like he really didn't want to." Sam crossed his arms and looked at the sky. "He was just afraid."

"Relationships are scary propositions."

"And who would know better than a man with five ex-wives."

Al chuckled and shook the link. "I love it when you remember the *really* important stuff."

"Yeah, me too." Sam watched the stars, waiting for them to brighten and blur as the familiar pull of Leap energy took him. It wasn't happening. "There's something else I'm supposed to do, isn't there, Al?"

"Maybe." Al shrugged. "Why don't you go back inside and see?"

When Sam walked in the ballroom, Gerda was talking on the pay phone near the entrance. She raised her eyebrows in greeting, throwing him a broad smile. "Marty's at the desk, signing in," she said, placing her hand over the mouthpiece. "We're up next." Onstage, one of the three jugglers tossed a machete in the air, caught it with his teeth, then bowed to the oohing, ahhing audience.

"You'll be happy to know, Sam, that Noah stays on with Rebecca, even though she takes a three-month sabbatical from teaching. He continues to work on getting her paperwork in order, which, as you know, is no small feat.'' Al winced as the jugglers tossed the machetes back and forth to one another. ''After a year, she takes an offer to teach voice at the Berklee School of Music in Boston, and refers Noah to the advertising firm that employed David Cullen. Seems Noah is pretty good at jingle writing. You remember this one—'Oh, if your drain's complainin'/ your pipes are strainin' to the max/get Clog B-Gone and just relax . . .' ''

Sam threw him a look of such bewilderment Al couldn't help but laugh. ''No, I guess you don't.'' Al hummed the rest of the ditty, as the jugglers ended their act by successfully juggling bowling balls with the machetes, then lifting their arms in unified triumph.

''And the crowd goes wild.'' Sam applauded as the cheers filled the room.

''Here.'' Gerda shoved the receiver into his hand. ''It's Rebecca. I called to check up on her. Talk to her a little, Noah. I don't like that she's alone. How do I look?''

''Like a million bucks.''

She patted him on the cheek, then ran to Gooshie, who was taking his place on the dance floor.

Sam looked at the receiver in his hand before placing it to his ear. ''Hello?''

''Hi, stranger.''

''You okay?''

''Getting better all the time.''

''Sounds like a song.''

''Beatles,'' she said. ''Sergeant Pepper.''

''Oh, yeah.''

The intro blared and Sam whipped around to see that Gerda was on, shimmying her hips and belting out her tune, while Gooshie did an unobtrusive soft shoe behind her.

''They make the cut, Sam.'' Al rocked on his heels, reading off the link. "They take first place in their category, second place all-around . . ."

Gerda let out a particularly powerful note, causing the crowd to cheer.

"Did you hear that applause?" Sam asked Rebecca.

"They're beat out by a guy who hums operatic arias through a comb and plastic wrap," Al said.

"Sssh!" Rebecca hushed Sam. "I'm trying to listen."

"I think I remember that guy," Al went on. "He was actually pretty amazing. The plastic wrap vibrated through the comb and sounded like a whole orchestra."

"She sounds great," Rebecca said.

"Hey . . . this is your first time at one of your students' auditions, isn't it?" The realization hit Sam the same time as the Leap energy.

"You know, you're right."

"Look at that." Sam said, his eyes drawn to the mirror ball, which was growing brighter and brighter with each languid turn. "You made it."

"Sssh!"

"Looks like you made it too, Sam." Al's voice entwined itself with the music.

"Again," Sam whispered, falling into the light, which flickered silver, gold, then blue, spinning . . . spinning away . . .

Away. For an instant he could taste every moment of the Leap, like a dying man reliving shards of the life from which he was reluctantly being drawn. Rebecca's kiss, Gerda's bombastic song stylings, frustration, grief, elation, Gooshie's reluctance, his slow path to acquiescence. Sam savored all of it, finding its taste bittersweet, delectable, like . . . the baking chocolate his mother used for her cookies. Yes. The rains used to play a gentle tattoo on the window, the rhythm making his eyelids droop as he did his homework at the kitchen table. His mother's kitchen smelled like cinnamon, nutmeg and cloves. She wore . . . she wore a pink apron sprayed with yellow daffodils. Setting a plate of cookies before him, she stroked his hair. The memories flowed easy now, like stones on a gently rolling stream. He paused at the bank, catching each one, clasping them to him as he drifted . . . drifted on to somewhen else . . .

CHAPTER THIRTY-SEVEN

"Each problem that I solved became a rule which served afterwards to solve other problems."
—Rene Descartes, "Discours de la Methode"

Al sat behind the wheel of the red Ferrari, which matched his shoes, *Kind of Blue* flowing like honey through all four speakers. He floated on the music and the car's lighter-than-air suspension, his recollections of the past Leap and his knowledge of the here and now ebbing and flowing in his head. The spiderweb crack in his windshield was gone. In this tentacle of time it had never existed. Perhaps the next time Sam Leaped, Al wouldn't have a Ferrari at all; maybe he'd have a Porsche, or a Cadillac or that VW minibus (no, please not *that*) he was once mortified to find in his parking space.

He was driving to Verdad to meet with the vacationing Gooshie again. Not to help him out of his doldrums, and not because Ziggy was acting like an insolent child, but because Gooshie had invited him to lunch to celebrate the grand opening of Marty's—the resort hotel Gerda had built with some financial help from the programmer and other investors.

Verdad had changed. No longer was it a haven for derelicts (and quite possibly it never had been in this timeline). Now it was a vacation vista. Quaint little restaurants and shops lined its cobblestone streets. Tourists armed with traveler's checks and American Express gold cards stayed in pricey bed and breakfasts with names like the Desert Inn or the Cactus Flower.

A year and a half ago, Gerda's notion to open a smaller version of her beloved Wildwood had struck a chord with Gooshie. After her performance on "You Can Be a Star," she'd been approached by several summer stock companies to perform on the road, offers which she was thrilled to accept. Over the next fifteen years she'd been Auntie Mame, Dolly Levi, Mama Rose—all the plum roles available for a woman "of a certain age." She socked her money away until she had enough to start the ball rolling toward seeing her final dream through.

She had traveled with Gooshie around Verdad and discovered a parcel of out-of-the-way acreage perfect for what they had in mind (it was rumored that prostitutes had wanted to build a "ranch" on this very spot, but the local government put their big boot into that one).

Al, of course, remembered that "ranch" and its madam with great amusement and lust. Only he could recall the time when the local government didn't grouse about either one's existence. He chomped on his cigar, feeling like something of a superior being with these alternate memories roaming through his head. Occasionally it could be disconcerting, but more often he considered it one of the perks of moonlighting as a time-leaping holographic image.

A valet approached Al's car at the entrance to the hotel parking lot. He was dressed in a red cap and button-down uniform, with MARTY's written in swirly calligraphy over his breast pocket.

"May I park your car, sir?" The man smiled, revealing a mouthful of straight white teeth. Al drew back in horror. His hand made an involuntary beeline for his keys, which were still in the ignition. He could clearly recall a time when the majority of the guy's teeth were nonexistent, and the remaining ones were interesting shades of yellow and black.

"Are you okay, sir?"

"Aren't you . . . Eddie?"

"Why, yes, sir." The man straightened his shoulders and touched the brim of his cap. "Eddie Tolinski, Parking Manager, at your service."

You, Eddie Tolinski, Parking Manager, would probably be horrified to learn that in another timeline you were a runty little desert weasel who got his kicks tossing beer bottles at Ferraris. "Uh . . . thanks for the offer, Eddie, but I'd just as soon tuck this little baby in myself."

"Yes, *sir.*"

Al steered the Ferrari through the lot, which was filled to near capacity, and found a spot at the side of the building. The resort was long and low, the same shade of pink as Madam's ranch had been. He spied an in-ground pool in the rear, where sun worshipers were either floating on rubber rafts or enjoying the outdoor buffet. Some of the extremely attractive women sported bikinis that looked more like two strands of dental floss. Al hitched an eyebrow, whistling in anticipation, knowing he'd have to give this area of the resort a more thorough investigation later on.

Still whistling, he strode into the lobby. The carpets were a soft shade of rose, the walls and registration desk brick red. Pink carnations were set in vases on white marble tables. He was about to try to find Gooshie's room, when the sound of familiar music stopped him.

He scratched his head and walked in the direction of the voice and piano. Peeking through the crack between two double doors marked BALLROOM, he spied an older, but no less redheaded and spry, Gerda on the stage. She was singing and demonstrating dance steps to a group of young women seated on risers behind her. After twirling on her toes and executing an extraordinarily agile high kick for someone her age, she beckoned for one of the women to do the same. Down from the risers drifted Al's dream—the former Madam of Verdad. Smiling, she efficiently mimicked Gerda's steps, her silver-light hair flowing behind her like an angel's. Swallowing hard, Al backed away from the door and groaned with desire. "Brrr!" He shuddered, shaking off his lust, then hurried away to find Gooshie.

Seated across from Gooshie, dipping one last piece of lobster in the seasoned butter, Al thought how surreal it was to experience firsthand the fruits of Sam's Leaping. Gerda hadn't lived past 1988 in the original history, but judging by the clandestine peek he'd taken of her downstairs, it seemed as if she had a barrelful of good years left.

He wished Sam could have been privy to Gerda's achievements, but Ziggy hadn't accessed the additional data in time for Al to relay it on the Leap. He lifted his glass and sipped. The mineral water was cold, tinged with lemon, just the way he liked it.

"So what do you think, Admiral?" Gooshie's skin was bronze and glowing; his paunch had all but disappeared. But he hadn't lost the cheezy mustache, the halitosis or the bookish demeanor. Those Gooshie-isms would remain, Al assumed, until the programmer breathed his last vile-smelling breath.

"It's all pretty incredible, Gooshie."

"She's not done yet, either." He said, eyes twinkling with admiration. "At the end of next year, if her money people's projections pan out, she's going to expand this place to twice its size."

"That's something." Al dabbed the butter off his chin with his linen napkin. "And this is your home away from home?"

"Yes, indeed, Admiral."

Al got up and strolled around the simple yet spacious room. The laptop on the desk was on, its screensaver a soaring *Starship Enterprise*. Al knew its connection to Ziggy was always open, just in case she was in need of some stimulating conversation or found herself missing her soul mate too much.

He ended up at the wall unit next to the stereo on the opposite side of the room. The unit housed five shelves, two filled with books, the others photos and photo albums. "Would you look at this," Al said more to himself than to Gooshie. Here was a framed photo of Gerda and Rebecca standing outside of the Berklee School of Music, another of Gooshie and Gerda accepting their awards on "You Can Be a Star," Gerda and Noah dancing at what was probably the Starlight Ballroom. Al lifted this photo from its frame and glanced at the date on the back. Turning it over again quickly, he peered more closely at Noah. The eyes were familiar, so inquisitive and bright, with just a touch of trepidation shining through. "Sam," Al said softly. He returned the photo to its frame and set it back on the shelf. Someday, he thought, swallowing hard against the lump in his throat, he would drive Sam up here in the Ferrari or Porsche or the minibus, and show him this photo. *This was you, buddy. Remember?*

Someday . . .

"What's wrong, Admiral?"

"Nothing, Gooshie." Al turned toward him and smiled. "Nothing at all."